For fourteen years now *Perry Rhodan* has been acknowledged to be the world's top-selling science fiction series. Originally published in magazine form in Germany, the series has now appeared in hardback and paperback in the States.

Over five hundred *Perry Rhodan* clubs exist on the Continent and *Perry Rhodan* fan conventions are held annually. The first *Perry Rhodan* film, *SOS From Outer Space*, has now been released in Europe.

The series has sold over 150 million copies in Europe alone.

Also available in the *Perry Rhodan* series

Kurt Mahr

Perry Rhodan 14
Venus in Danger

Futura Publications Limited
An Orbit Book

An Orbit Book

First published in Great Britain in 1976
by Futura Publications Limited

Copyright © Ace Books 1972

An Ace Book, by arrangement with
Arthur Moewig Verlag

This series was created by Karl-Herbert Scheer
and Walter Ernsting, translated by Wendayne Ackerman
and edited by Frederik Pohl and Forrest J. Ackerman

ISBN 0 8600 7892 2

This English edition is dedicated to Edmond Hamilton.
Captain Future Himself Who Was Already Out There
In The Universe In The '20s

Printed in Great Britain by
Hazell Watson & Viney Ltd
Aylesbury, Bucks

Futura Publications Limited
110 Warner Road
Camberwell, London SE5

CHAPTER ONE

LOST—ONE LUSTRUM!

Perry Rhodan was the first to pull out. Out of the shock of hyper-transition.

Around him the circular command center of the super-spaceship *Stardust II* took on form once again: switch consoles, control panels, videoscreens, chairs and tables emerged from the gray contourless state of hytrans and regained their familiar shape.

Moments later the relay signal from the positroni-computer began to function again and Rhodan could study the picture on the observation screen and assess the situation.

Reginald Bell, First Officer and co-pilot, had collapsed over his console. Groaning, he straightened up and looked about with astonished eyes. 'Where . . . what—? Oh! It's always the same.'

During transition the nerve-functions in the human body were reduced to minimum. The end of the transition always came like the awakening from a stupor or semi-consciousness.

'Position!' Rhodan requested in a firm voice. 'Data check and set course for normal flight.'

Bell started to move. Rhodan's orders stirred up

the other members of the crew who were leaning back in contour chairs or holding fast to table edges, trying to overcome the shock of hyperjump.

Gradually the command center came alive once more and hummed with activity. Reports came in, quick and precise.

'Position: $R = 6 \times 10^{12}$, Phi $= 81°21'$, Theta $= 113°$.'

The recording graphometer, with its characteristic scratchy noise, identified the position of the ship as a red dot on the insert card.

'Data deviations: R minus 10^8, Phi $+ 11''$, Theta none.'

A fleeting smile crossed Perry's face.

'This is as close as you can get,' Bell said.

'Flight course data requested,' came the voice of a navigation officer, adding, still a little shaky: 'Here they come—!'

*

Stardust II was located at a distance of 3·5 billion miles from the Sun and was moving into the solar system on a straight line slightly inclined to the mean plane of the planets' orbits.

The ship had emerged from hyperspace at 75% of the velocity of light. On Rhodan's instructions the speed was increased to 95%.

Earth was situated on the far side of the Sun, Venus and Mars in front. According to calculations the ship should pass the Sun on a course 24 million miles distant.

The transition had been successful, the range of error unexpectedly small. There seemed no reason – and therefore nobody took the trouble to check – to verify the date on the calendar.

*

'Calling Gobi headquarters!'

The radio officer switched on the telecom and adjusted the transmitter to the energy output required to reach the Earth.

'I'd like to talk to Col. Freyt,' Rhodan added.

He watched the young officer as he manipulated the intricate set.

Everybody is tired, Rhodan thought. It is time that we get some rest. The Wanderer episode took a lot out of the boys.

From time to time he glanced at the large entrance hatch. Reginald Bell noticed it and remarked with a faint smile, 'They won't see anybody?'

Rhodan shook his head. 'It's better this way. I can't help but feel a little guilty in the presence of the Arkonides.'

Bell dismissed this with a gesture of his hand. 'It's not your fault. It was *his* decision that neither Thora nor Khrest nor any other Arkonide should receive the treatment under the Physiotron. *He* . . .'

'Forget it!' Rhodan vehemently interrupted. '*He*,

7

he, always *he!* One would think that you're beginning to believe that *he* is God Himself!'

At the same time the hoarse voice of the young radio technician exclaimed in panic: 'I don't get any answer from Earth, sir!'

Without further ado Rhodan put the thought, which just now had excited him so much, out of his mind. With two quick steps he was at the telecom set and examined the controls.

'There's nothing wrong with the telecom,' the officer said, 'if that's what you suspect. It functions all right and the call is getting through as you can see from the echo. They don't respond on Earth, sir.'

Rhodan could see it for himself. 'Let me try it,' he told the technician.

The young officer gave his seat to Rhodan, who hastily repeated the call on the transmitter. He saw the green dot reflected on the oscillator screen and waited.

Nothing.

The Earth remained silent.

Rhodan had trouble hiding his anxiety.

He tried again. He pushed the automatic call button with determination.

There was the green reflex and then a flickering on the picture screen.

Col. Freyt's face was suspicious at first but smiling with radiant eyes as soon as he recognized that he was talking to Rhodan. 'Chief, it's you!'

Rhodan demonstrated little patience for a big welcome scene. 'What's the matter? Why don't you make a proper report? We had to call you three times before you answered.'

Freyt froze. His smile disappeared but his eyes were still beaming.

'Col. Freyt in Galacto-City!' he reported. 'I didn't answer your first calls because I suspected a trap, sir!'

'A trap?'

'Yes, sir. An attempt to locate our position. I had orders to use extreme caution pertaining to hyper-radio.'

Rhodan nodded. 'I know, but didn't you expect us to return around this time?'

'No, sir. How was I to know that you'd have such difficulties coming back?'

'Difficulties?' Rhodan shouted. 'It was the smoothest return I ever had!'

But Freyt continued, undeterred: 'In order to avoid any misunderstanding it would perhaps have been better, sir, if you had given me some more information about the current situation, providing of course that the circumstances permitted it since your last call.'

Rhodan frowned. 'Listen, Freyt, how many calls do I have to make in a month to keep you abreast of the situation. I believe . . .'

9

'A month!' Freyt exclaimed. 'Have you lost track of the time?'

Rhodan was startled 'What do you mean? This is the 29th of January and I called you last December.'

Freyt looked as if he had begun to doubt Rhodan's sanity. Rhodan could tell from the expression of his narrowed eyes that something must have happened in the meantime which he had missed. 'Today, sir,' Freyt said as quietly as he could manage, 'is the 24th of May; nearly five years have passed since your last call.'

The conversation had been conducted loud enough so that a few of the attending officers could overhear it.

Rhodan could feel the sudden, breathless quiet. He thought of a number of implausible explanations while he stared into Freyt's face and waited till his men started to stir again behind him. 'Well,' he finally said in such an impassive tone that it made his listeners wonder whether he cared at all about missing nearly half a decade, 'somewhere along the line we seem to have lost a few years. And how did you get along in the meantime, Freyt?'

Freyt breathed a sigh of relief. He had been afraid that complications had occurred. 'Not too well, sir,' he answered truthfully. 'Here on Earth the conviction has spread that hope for your return must be abandoned. Only the Eastern Bloc considers this an advantage whereas the Asiatic Federation and NATO still endeavor to attain a true world government. A new government has taken over the Eastern Bloc by force and since that time the prospects are that the third world war will come sooner or later. So far I've not tried to influence the course of developments because . . .'

Rhodan waved his hand. 'It's alright, Freyt. We'll have landed in less than an hour and then we'll see what is to be done.' He ended the conversation and swiveled around with his chair so that he faced Bell.

Bell seemed rather perplexed. 'Where have we been all this time?' he asked.

Rhodan shrugged his shoulders. 'We'll have to rack our brains about that later. Perhaps time on Wanderer was different from ours. What is of the foremost importance right now is the fact that affairs on Earth are not what they should be.'

*

A few minutes later the *Stardust* passed the orbit of Mars at a point 12 million miles away from the planet.

As the ship was about to cross the path of the Earth, which was at this time located at the other side of the sun, Rhodan received a call from the range finder section. The voice which made the report sounded puzzled. 'Unknown material objects detected, sir!'

'Position?'

The man stated the position as requested and added:

'This is on the opposite side of Venus, sir.'

'Continue your observation!' Rhodan ordered. 'Report to me as soon as you have found out more about it!'

He switched the telecom set off and looked at the observation screen in front of him.

Foreign objects in the vicinity of Venus!

Nothing was more valuable and irreplaceable for the New Power and Rhodan than the base on Venus containing the most powerful defense installations and the gigantic positronic brain.

Did the presence of foreign objects indicate that somebody was preparing to land on Venus?

Rhodan smiled grimly. He had believed that he could come home triumphantly. He had defeated a terrible enemy, the Topides; he had found the secret of eternal life, acquired a wealth of knowledge surpassing even that of the two Arkonides Khrest and Thora, and had on the planet Wanderer received the assurance that mankind was destined to rule the Galaxy.

These would have been more than enough reasons to accord a rousing welcome to Rhodan!

Once again the range finder officer appeared on the telecom and announced very excitedly: 'Observed at least 400 separate objects ahead of us resembling spaceships. Fairly small. Volume of each object about

100,000 cubic feet. Approaching Venus. Appear to be headed for landing.'

Rhodan jumped up.

'We'll change course, gentlemen!' he said brusquely. 'We'll stop on Venus. All-out alert goes into immediate effect.'

Without looking he pulled down the lever of the alarm signal. The wail of sirens filled the long corridors and all the departments of the gigantic ship.

The *Stardust* had returned home but what they had to do first was to lower the shields from their guns and show the enemy what he was in for with his challenge.

*

Col. Freyt could give no information about the sighted objects. Rhodan notified him about his change of plans as the *Stardust* veered to the new course. Freyt was displeased but he realized that the base on Venus was of paramount importance.

No suspicious movement in space had been observed at the Gobi headquarters and they had no idea who was responsible for the activity around Venus.

Only Rhodan had an inkling of the true facts although they seemed as yet rather preposterous; but there was no other explanation. Freyt could not have failed to detect an armada of 400 ships invading the solar system from outer space.

Ergo, they did not come from outer space!

Rhodan ordered Col. Freyt to stand by.

*

Gen. Tomisenkov watched as his tent was pitched. He was dressed lightly as the climatic conditions on this world necessitated. He wore short pants and a shirt with opened collar. The epaulets with the insignia of his rank had slid down over his collarbone.

Tomisenkov took off his cap and wiped the sweat from his forehead with his hand. Then he looked at his aide: 'Miserable weather, isn't it?'

The aide quickly agreed that the weather was indeed disgusting.

The latter came from Sevastopol where the weather was not much different in summer. But Gen. Tomisenkov had spent the greatest part of his life in Ochotsk, and in Ochotsk people were freezing even in July.

It was not advisable to contradict Gen. Tomisenkov, whatever the subject might be.

'But we'll soon have finished our business here and then we won't have to wipe the sweat from our brows every minute.'

He wiped again.

At this moment a man with a sheet of paper in his hand rushed out from behind the half-erected tents. 'A message!' he shouted from afar, 'a message for the general!'

Tomisenkov turned around. 'Give me that!' he

barked. He perused the short message. The aide saw him get red in the face. 'Why are you wasting time running around with papers?' he yelled at the messenger. 'Why didn't you start shooting?'

The messenger stood at attention.

'Run, man, run!' Tomisenkov bellowed. 'Tell them to shoot down that thing!'

The messenger took off in a hurry. Tomisenkov took his aide by the arm and pulled him over. 'They've spotted something,' he explained. 'At first they thought it was a celestial body because it was so big; but when it executed deliberate movements they wanted me to tell them what to do.'

He looked slyly at his aide: 'Do you know what it is?'

'No, General!'

'Then I'll tell you. You've heard the stories about that American Major Perry Rhodan flying around in space in superships? Don't you remember him? I believe he got wind of our Venus expedition a little sooner than I suspected and now he wants to get into our hair.'

The aide blanched.

'Perry Rhodan?'

Tomisenkov nodded eagerly.

'That's what it looks like. I've always wanted to meet him. Apparently the time has finally come.'

The ground began to drone. Farther ahead in the

jungle eight defense rockets shot into the cloudy Venusian sky.

Tomisenkov laughed. 'Won't he be surprised to get such a warm reception!'

*

'Landing in four minutes! Protective screens?'
'Check, sir!'

Rhodan looked around. There were only four men left in the command center with him and Bell. The other officers had taken up their posts with the crew and at the battle stations.

The observation screens depicted the deck of clouds above Venus. It was getting darker.

Only the infra-red and microwave range finders reflected the surface of the hot jungle planet. A river delta which seemed to approach rapidly toward the observer, a coastline, a clearing in the jungle—

'Attack rockets!'

A bright flash on the screen, blue-white and painful for the unprotected eyes. They failed to hear a sound. The mighty ship kept following its course unperturbably.

Bell reported impassively: 'Nuclear warhead, fission type, yield one megaton TNT!' Then he turned around and asked with curiosity: 'Well, what was that?'

Rhodan grinned in amusement. There was a second flash on the screen. 'Who would shoot with such old-fashioned explosive missiles at a spaceship?'

He left it to Bell to figure out the answer. Then *he* called the range finder and was informed that the trajectory of the rockets had been traced back to its point of origin. They came from the northern polar continent, close above the coast.

The battle stations waited in vain for the order to fire their guns. Rhodan decided on a different action.

He took over the *Stardust* by manual steering, descended with the ship almost to the surface of the ocean and continued racing with high speed toward the coast of the northern continent.

Rhodan watched the surface of the water flit by and the bluish mantle of light enveloping the protective screen of the ship. This latter effect was the result of the swift movement of the vessel and the impact of the air molecules on the screen causing them to be ionized and to radiate.

Under the dark sky of the Venus afternoon the ship approached the far-stretched line of the unbroken coast behind which the jungle began.

CHAPTER TWO

DISCOVERY ON VENUS

Tomisenkov cursed.

'Fire another salvo!' he yelled at the battery officer. 'No matter what kind of a defense screen they have, it's bound to collapse if we keep up our bombardment.'

He was right in principle. The defense screen was not completely immune to penetration if it was overloaded. However, Tomisenkov had no idea when the load for the *Stardust*'s protective screen became excessive.

His hundreds of nuclear rockets were insufficient and if he had had thousands of the same type he would not have had enough.

The battery officer proceeded to comply with his orders. He issued short and precise commands through his little transmitter to the servicemen at the rocket positions.

Just then the radar technicians reported another surprise.

'The enemy ship is coming toward us, General! Velocity about nine miles per second. It's as big as . . . !'

The fiery sphere grew bigger and bigger and when

Tomisenkov thought it was about to pass over his camp, he realized how he had misjudged its size.

The sphere kept growing second by second, reached the camp looking like a fire-spitting mountain and shot past—

And pandemonium followed.

Tomisenkov's eardrums failed to function after the first shockwave crashed over him. He could no longer see because his eyes were blinded. But he unmistakably felt the irresistible force which swept him from his feet, carried him aloft and tossed him away. He suffered a violent whiplash across his face as he was pushed across a wire and down onto the ground, hitting a sharp edge with a painful blow. The impact took his breath away. He made a desperate attempt to get up on his knees. Then he lost consciousness.

He had no idea how much time had passed when he woke up again. His wristwatch was gone.

He got up in spite of the jabbing pain in his chest, cautiously took a deep breath and looked around.

What he saw surpassed his worst fears.

The camp had ceased to exist.

The jungle had changed. A mile-wide swatch stretched across the jungle from the south, crossed the camp, the rocket emplacements and the landing field of the spacefleet, continuing toward the north.

A straight line, as if drawn by an oversize steamroller.

He controlled his emotions, realizing that the

situation was too dangerous to permit delving into his own feelings. He slowly began to move his bulky figure and set out to look for the people who had been with him in the small clearing before the disaster struck.

The battery officer was dead. But the aide showed signs of life after Tomisenkov shook him thoroughly.

Finally he opened his eyes and stared utterly confused at the general.

'Get up!' Tomisenkov shouted.

Although Tomisenkov understood his own words, the aide shook his head questioningly and put both hands on his ears.

Tomisenkov had a remedy. He pressed his forehead against that of the aide and repeated: 'I told you to get up!'

It worked. The vibrating skulls transmitted the sound. The aide understood and jumped to his feet.

Tomisenkov made a sweeping gesture with his arms across the camp and strode away. His aide walked in the opposite direction.

The search for survivors commenced.

The track of the storm was six miles wide. Down the middle extended a mile-wide fire-scarred stretch like an open wound. The soil was a molten mass and radiated an unbearable heat. For the time being it was impossible for Tomisenkov to cross over to the other side of the burned swath in his search for his men.

What had happened? This was the question up-permost in everybody's mind.

The only one who had a clear idea about it was Tomisenkov. But he had other problems to tackle than to enlighten his men how badly he had under-estimated Rhodan. The camp – or rather what was left of it – had to be transported to some other place. Tomisenkov was afraid that Rhodan would return and he was not yet convinced that he was forced to capitulate.

The jungles on Venus were vast. They offered hiding places for hundreds of divisions, impossible to detect by the adversary.

Tomisenkov proved his talent for organization. Although 6000 of his men were so badly hurt that they could not move by themselves and despite the fact that it took three times as long as usual to explain his commands to the men with deaf ears, the transfer was on the way two hours after the catastrophe.

Those who were most seriously wounded were loaded into the ships which were still intact. The other casualties were carried on make-shift stretchers through the jungle.

Instructions were left for the soldiers who were still on the other side of the scorched red hot strip to let them know where to follow.

Tomisenkov's goal was a chain of mountains situated in the northwest. The distance was no more than 120 miles but Tomisenkov estimated that they would require at least a week of Terrestrial time to reach it, due to their encumbered mode of traveling.

He was the last to leave the abandoned camp with his aide and a few other high officers. The departure had proceeded smoothly and had taken only 10 hours. In the meantime their hearing had been partially restored and they were able to converse again, albeit by shouting very loudly.

When Tomisenkov noticed that curiosity and anxiety were gaining the upper hand among his men, he decided to break his silence and tried to dispel their fears by explaining the true circumstances to the officers.

'I suppose you have all noticed the sphere,' he yelled. 'There can be no doubt about it that it was the spaceship which Perry Rhodan uses for his famed expeditions throughout the universe.'

'But it must have been half a mile big!' somebody interjected.

Tomisenkov cocked his head.

'Just about, yes. What we've experienced was not a special weapon. Our radar station reported at the last moment that the ship was approaching us at nine miles per second. This is about three miles per second faster than a meteor streaking into the Earth's atmosphere from outer space. There is not enough time for the air to circumvent such a fast body. The air becomes compressed to such a degree that its molecules are made to radiate or even become ionized. As a result of the high compression of the air the temperature also rises momentarily to a formidable heat.'

He pointed in the general direction of the scorched lane and continued to shout: 'There you can see the effect! We might ask,' he went on, 'how does Rhodan make the air glow without setting his own ship on fire? We don't know the exact answer to this question. All we know is that his ship is protected by a high-energy screen which presumably is also capable of absorbing the destructive side effects of such a maneuver.'

He paused to wait for questions which did not come.

'I want to stress that we must advance as fast as possible,' Tomisenkov exhorted his officers. 'Rhodan won't keep us waiting very long. He knows very well what is at stake on Venus. We intend to give him a warm reception!'

*

Nine miles per second is too fast for the human eye to perceive details and to record differentiations.

Rhodan was unable to tell when and where the *Stardust* had swooped across his opponent's camp. However, the automatic cameras had recorded the flight and it was thus made easy to ascertain the pertinent observations.

There was still a lot of guesswork on board the vessel about the identity of the invader who had succeeded in landing on Venus and getting so perilously close to the vital Venus base.

The only one among them who could have provided the information remained silent. Rhodan gradually slowed down the speed of his mighty ship and headed in a gentle curve toward the rocky slopes of the mountain where the base was situated.

However at a distance of 300 miles from the base the *Stardust* was suddenly stopped. Although the effect was very strong it did not damage the vessel. The gravity neutralizers absorbed the shock of braking and the sphere came to rest above the steaming jungle within a few seconds.

Feeling a little tired, Rhodan leaned back in his chair. Apprehension was growing around him. Reginald Bell ran from one instrument to the other. The radio operator tried frantically to transmit the hyperwave code signal to the positronic brain inside the fortress, and the Third Officer queried the Technical Control Center whether any of the machinery was out of commission.

None of these measures brought any results.

Finally Rhodan issued the command:

'Prepare for landing!'

Bell stared at him incredulously.

'What's wrong? Why can't we get in?'

'Because we've been too cautious,' Rhodan answered quietly.

He let it go at that without further elaborating his

answer. Rhodan watched attentively as the *Stardust* descended toward the ground. The dense, 40-yard-high tree cover caved in like parched grass under the 800-yard-diameter sphere. The hydraulic landing supports were extended and sank deep into the soft ground of the jungle. A red lamp lit up on the control panel and a reassuring voice announced:

'We've touched down!'

Rhodan got up and directed his officers by intercom: 'Will all officers please come to the command center. I have a statement to make.'

His order was followed immediately. The command center was filled within a minute. The *Stardust* had a crew of 500 men, 40 of them officers. In addition there were a number of mutants with the rank of officer in accordance with the regulations of the New Power.

Rhodan's disclosure that the *Stardust* had been absent for four and a half years elicited considerable amazement. He refrained from offering any explanations and merely announced the bare fact.

He went on to convey the information he had received from Col. Freyt about the political developments on Earth.

'When we return to Earth,' he said, 'we'll find that the situation there is very different from what we remember. The interval of four and a half years sufficed for some self-seeking persons to usurp power and to contravene our plans for mankind. We'll have to see to it that no harm will come to Earth through these misadventures.

'But first of all we've another problem to deal with. All our plans for improving mankind's condition and for Earth taking its place in the Galaxy are virtually dependent on our ability to maintain access to the planet Wanderer anytime in a period up to 10,000 years. We know a fragment of its orbit and have thus enough data for the super-positronic brain in the Venus fortress to compute the trajectory in the distant future.

'In any case it is one of our most essential tasks to feed the available information as soon as possible into the positronic brain since the passage of time makes all calculations much more difficult.

'This necessity has become even more urgent now that an ambitious foe has landed on Venus with the intention of taking over our base.'

He paused and closed his eyes as if he had to consider his next words carefully.

'The positronic has been programmed in such a manner that it will commit no harm to humans. I've chosen my instructions with the thought in mind that some accident might happen to one of us on our flight to Venus which could prevent us from transmitting the agreed code signal. The previous procedure was such that the brain would have unfailingly repulsed and destroyed us on the spot. This had to be avoided.

'I admit frankly that it never occurred to me that

people from Earth would attempt to invade Venus against our will.

'Yet this is exactly what has happened. The numerous slow-moving objects, which our range finder registered during our flight in the vicinity of Venus' path, are no doubt nuclear spaceships built on Earth by someone other than the New Power. The attack rockets which have greeted us also point to the fact that the incursion originated on Earth. And finally, the fact that the positronic has permitted the landing is the best proof for my assumptions.

'Judging from Col. Freyt's report, there can't be the slightest doubt that a huge fleet of spaceships was dispatched from the Eastern Bloc to take possession of Venus.

'The positronic brain has taken one more action. The bombardment of the *Stardust* by the nuclear missiles was an occurrence which was classified in the memory banks as "unusual and threatening". The positronic brain had my strict instructions to seal off the entire area hermetically in such a case and to prevent anybody from entering the base.

'I'm now aware that it was a case of unwarranted prudence on my part. However, I submit that there was no one among us with fanciful enough imagination to predict such a possibility.

'The unfortunate fact remains that we too can't penetrate the protective field of the base. We must now endeavour to summarily eliminate the threat of the encroaching army and to demonstrate thereby for the positronic brain that the hazard has ceased to exist.'

Rhodan looked sternly at his officers.

'I repeat that we have to act swiftly. It is a simple conclusion that we've only three weeks of Terrestrial time left before it becomes impossible for the positronic brain to calculate the entire trajectory from the known segment.

'Please advise the men under your command of the new situation and stand by for my instructions. Thank you, gentlemen!'

The *Stardust* faced an arduous task which was, however, by no means beyond solution.

Everybody had left the command center except Rhodan, Bell and two other officers who supervised operations and communications.

Bell shook his head.

'To be honest,' he said in a vexed tone, 'I can't understand you. Do you think it's wise to admit in front of the men that you've made a mistake?'

They sat in front of the pilot's console. The two other officers were far enough in the background so that they could talk freely.

Rhodan laughed. 'Why not? I did make an error, didn't I?'

'I wouldn't call it an error. They would all have considered you a fool if you had taken precautions at that time against such an unlikely eventuality as the Eastern Bloc making an assault on Venus with an armada.'

Rhodan shrugged his shoulders. 'They did it anyway. No, it was my fault. I should have taken all contingencies into consideration, no matter how farfetched.'

Bell stretched out his upturned hands. 'Well, if that's how you feel about it; but there's something else I fail to understand.'

'What's that?'

'Freyt must've been well aware of the detrimental developments on Earth. Why didn't he do anything about it?'

Rhodan looked dismayed. 'I must take the blame for that too,' he replied. 'Freyt was under the influence of a hypnotic block. He was not in a position to interfere with the political events on Earth. I imposed this hypnotic block on his mind because I couldn't be absolutely sure that he wouldn't fall victim to political ambitions during my absence. The enormous technical means of the New Power which were at his disposal might have tempted him too much. That's why I had to impose some restrictions. Therefore, he was unable to take any steps to contain the Eastern Bloc when the government was overthrown and inimical policies were instituted there.'

Reginald Bell nodded quietly in agreement.

'Well,' he said after a while, 'who would have thought that we would be out of the picture for four and a half years? I'm sure you'd done it differently.'

Rhodan traced the pattern of the floor with the tip of his boot. 'Don't try to find excuses for me,' he told Bell. 'It was a mistake that I made all decisions in my own head with my limited logical powers. In future I'll have to consult more frequently with the positronic brain. It's more reliable and rejects any preconceived ideas.'

Bell looked at him with a serious expression. 'And what are you going to do about the invasion fleet? Why don't we simply rub it out?'

Rhodan answered hesitantly: 'In the first place I'm reluctant to rub people out and, secondly, it's too late to accomplish it. If the commander of the fleet is worth his salt, he must have evacuated his last position immediately and we're going to have trouble to locate him again in these jungles.'

Bell listened attentively.

'Besides, he'll have dispersed his soldiers so far apart that a concentrated bombardment would be useless. Is that what you mean?'

Rhodan nodded in assent.

'Exactly.'

Bell thought for a moment.

'So we'll have to fight a little in the jungle?'

Rhodan smiled.

'I'll be happy if it turns out to be a little fight,' he said pensively.

CHAPTER THREE

CONVERSATION WITH KHREST

Rhodan's candor toward his men gained the opposite result from what Reginald Bell had expected.

For the first time in the history of the New Power there had been occasion for Rhodan to admit a mistake since it was the only one for which he was responsible up to now.

Whereas the entire crew had always admired his superior knowledge and his outstanding qualities, they now felt that he needed them as well since he was not only a genius but very human like everybody else.

Their admiration had generally kept them at a certain distance from Rhodan but now their feelings were augmented by a strong sense of togetherness and unity.

Each order Rhodan gave for preparing the action against the invading army was carried out without delay and very conscientiously. Everything went like clockwork. Two hours after they had set down, the pictures which had been filmed during their earlier flight had been evaluated and Rhodan had worked out the tactics which he had to follow. It required two more hours of reconnaissance to determine how Gen. Tomisenkov had reacted to the initial blow and seven hours after their landing a preliminary task force of 50 men with equipment and weapons was ready to leave the ship.

Rhodan took personal command of the mission.

But before he left he had a talk with the two Arkonides, Thora and Khrest.

*

The purpose which had brought the two Arkonides to this part of the Galaxy in one of the last research cruisers the decadent Arkonide race had managed to build, was the search for eternal life. They were seeking a world whose inhabitants knew the secret of cell conservation.

The research cruiser was forced to make an emergency landing on the moon just at the time when the first atomic rocket to the moon was launched from Earth.

This course of events inevitably led to their meeting on the moon and from then on the astronauts on the old *Stardust*; Rhodan, Bell and Dr. Manoli; banded together for better or worse with the two surviving Arkonides of the destroyed exploration cruiser.

On their return to Earth the superior weapons of the Arkonides enabled them to prevent the outbreak of the third world war after they had established themselves as the New Power in the Gobi desert.

As far as Rhodan was concerned their coopera-
tion was very useful from the outset. He was aiming
for such lofty goals as unification of mankind and
security for Terra's position in the Galaxy. The Arkonides and their far-advanced technology had arrived at a very auspicious moment to help Rhodan.

On the other hand Khrest and Thora were at first
more motivated by the advantages Rhodan presented
to them for their rescue than by pure sympathy.
Rhodan was an extremely energetic man. After he
had absorbed the knowledge of the Arkonides by way
of hypno-training, he would be capable of creating
manufacturing facilities to construct a long-range
spaceship of the Arkonide type. With such a ship
Khrest and Thora could either continue their search
for the world of eternal life or return to their home
on Arkon.

In the interim a few complications had developed.
Alien intruders had attacked Earth and had to be
repulsed by the New Power. Later the New Power
became involved in a war in the Vegan system during
which they had the good fortune to capture *Stardust II* from their opponents. The possession of this
formidable spaceship enticed them to undertake a
long and tortuous journey through the universe to
locate the mysterious place Thora and Khrest had
set out to find years ago.

At the end of their perilous trip they came to Wanderer – the Planet of Eternal Life.

It was an artificial world which was put by its creator into a peculiar orbit around 30 different solar systems.

Rhodan discovered the precious secret and learned at the same time that the history of the Arkonides had run its course on the cosmic clock of the universe. The Arkonides were denied the treatment for cell conservation and the gift of eternal life was withheld from them.

Khrest and Thora had put Rhodan on the track of the secret and now that they had found it together they were refused the goal of their desire.

The secret had been granted to Rhodan – the heir of the Galactic Imperium.

*

Khrest sat alone in his cabin. He leaned back in a flexible contour chair and stared at the ceiling. He did not move when Rhodan entered.

Rhodan went over to his side. 'I don't think,' Rhodan said softly and with compassion, 'it is very sensible to sink into melancholy.' He spoke in the Arkonide language.

Khrest remained silent for a while. Then he turned his head toward Rhodan and looked at him with a serious expression.

'You can't imagine,' he answered, 'how disappointing this failure is for me and all Arkonides. All we lacked for ultimate perfection was the secret of eternal life, nothing else. It is a cruel blow to learn that we were rejected and denied attainment of the highest phase of evolution.'

Rhodan vainly searched for words. He sat down beside Khrest. 'I'm leaving the ship,' he said earnestly. 'Somebody has infiltrated Venus and is giving us trouble.'

Khrest raised his white eyebrows but gave no other sign of surprise or anxiety.

'I don't know how long we'll stay out there,' Rhodan continued. 'That's why I'd like to ask a favor of you.'

Khrest managed a faint smile. 'Are you sure,' he asked, 'that I'll ever get up from this chair and overcome my depression?'

Rhodan nodded. 'Quite sure. Would you please keep an eye on Thora? She has suffered so much from the traumatic experience on Wanderer and you know how impulsive she is.'

Khrest kept smiling. 'Of course I'll look out for her,' he assured Rhodan. 'I haven't seen her since we left but I'll go right over to visit her.' With these words he got up. 'I wish you good luck,' he said to Rhodan. 'I hope you'll come back alright.'

Rhodan nodded again.

Two minutes later he entered the exit hatch and gave his men last minute instructions.

The corps of 50 men consisted of four groups. Rhodan had assigned the command of the other groups to his trusty officers Maj. Deringhouse, Maj. Nyssen and Lt. Tanner.

Each man was wearing an Arkonide transport suit which was a multi-purpose outfit provided with an artificial gravity generator enabling the wearer to move through the air. In addition it incorporated a tiny electromagnetic set to produce a deflection field which imparted quasi-hydromechanical qualities to the surrounding medium so that the propagation of lightwaves was directed in streamlines around the field thereby making the man inside invisible.

Each group had three of the versatile Arkonide vehicles which moved with equal ease on land, in the air and through water.

The men were equipped with the usual weapons. Only the officers carried small psycho-beamers.

'The enemy is on the march,' Rhodan pointed out. 'We believe that we know his destination but we'll have to keep in constant communication with the *Stardust* to check his advance.

'We're planning to conduct an old-fashioned jungle war. Whoever is in charge on the other side must know that our equipment is far superior and will act accordingly.

'He'll widely disperse his soldiers and use guerrilla tactics in order to prevent us from utilizing our more efficient weapons.

'Nevertheless, we must bring our mission to a quick and decisive conclusion. We don't have much time to spare. Do the best you can!'

*

Gen. Tomisenkov soon found out that he had considerably underestimated the difficulties involved in this march.

For two hours Lt. Chanikadse marched ahead of Tomisenkov on the path hacked out of the jungle by the forward troop. He was trying to keep the twigs from hitting the general in the face.

At the beginning of the third hour, just as Chanikadse was busy clearing a vine out of the way, a hideous white worm as thick as a man's thigh had slithered with amazing suppleness and speed onto the path, wrapped itself around the lieutenant and dragged him into the jungle.

Before Tomisenkov and his officers could come to his aid, the huge worm had reeled off about 60 feet of its repulsive colorless length. They started to shoot like mad with their automatic pistols at the remaining 60 feet but their bullets did little to bother the worm.

Chanikadse was lost. Tomisenkov forbade any pursuit of the worm. He did not want to risk losing more men in the treacherous jungle.

Half an hour later they heard a droning rhythmic

noise from a westerly direction. The aide thought it was an earthquake.

After another hour they saw what it was, or rather they could approximately reconstruct the picture. An animal of gargantuan size had crossed the narrow pathway in the jungle and set down one of its legs exactly in the middle of the path. It left a circular impression of 15 feet in diameter. Inside they found some torn remnants of uniforms and the soil was drenched with blood. Tomisenkov had no way of knowing how many of his men had met their death here.

Two miles farther the trail took a sharp turn to the south and led around a narrow but long forest lake. The detour was too long for one of his officers. He waded into the water and began to swim.

When he had about three quarters of his way behind him, he had to avoid a strange obstacle lying motionlessly like a colorful opalescent carpet on the surface of the water. The officer swam in a wide curve around it but the carpet started to move and follow him. The swimmer did not notice it at first. Only when Tomisenkov and the other onlookers shouted warnings was his attention drawn to the menace behind him. The man tried to reach the shore with a furious crawl but at the spot where he first treaded ground the carpet caught up with him. The water began to swirl and another of Tomisenkov's men vanished. The carpet underwent an odd change.

Instead of looking colorful and spread out over the water, it turned into a gray and solid lump which overpowered its far weaker victim.

The lump retreated with astounding speed to the deep water of the lake where it went under with the officer, never to be seen again.

*

Beyond the burned out and molten strip of land the *Stardust* had drawn across the jungle in a straight line, a few men of Tomisenkov's rocket defense detachment remained alive.

Originally more than 200 men of the outer space assault division had been part of the defense detachment. Only 28 of them had survived.

Maj. Lysenkov had assumed command of the last 28 soldiers. He was a fairly young man who was very eager to show his men that he was in control of the situation.

The eardrums of the group to the east of the devastated path had also been damaged to a great extent by the noise of the thundering *Stardust*. Lysenkov had to exchange written notes with his men, as he failed to hit upon Tomisenkov's excellent idea.

After a few hours had elapsed and Lysenkov thought it was safe to use the portable transmitter, he tried to get in touch with the general. Up to this time the 28 had done nothing except treat their injuries, check the radioactivity of the molten mass and measure the temperature of the molten terrain.

Tomisenkov did not answer nor did anyone else react to the call.

Lysenkov was at a loss to understand why his call did not get through and it took quite some time until he came to the conclusion that Tomisenkov had probably abandoned the camp and that he must have left some information behind as to his whereabouts.

Lysenkov did not relish the thought that he would have to wait until the burned-out stretch had cooled off safely. It was now 180:00 o'clock local time and it would get dark in 10 to 12 hours.

Lysenkov had taken part in the fruitless bombardment of the hostile ship. He had a fair idea of what had happened although he had no explanation for a number of the details. He expected that the opponent would attack for a second time after the pause and issued instructions to prepare the launching ramps for the rockets.

CHAPTER FOUR

JUNGLE CAPTIVES

Then they waited.

Maj. Deringhouse was supposed to search both sides of the demolished strip for any remnants of the troops from the deserted military camp.

Deringhouse had left his unit with two of his vehicles and proceeded south close above the tree-tops of the forest.

The western half of the camp was desolate and empty except for the bodies of those who had fallen victim to the tornado. Then he passed at an altitude of 1500 feet over the dividing lane. As the sun was about to set, the two vehicles landed next to one of the overturned and twisted rocket ramps on the ground.

Deringhouse examined the ramp but the only note-worthy observations about it were the Cyrillic letters of the markings on the little electronic switch panel – proof that the expedition had originated from the Eastern Bloc.

He further reflected upon the fact that, unless the ramp had been thrown here by air pressure from the explosion, it had been set up in a clearing in the underbrush with a minimum required for a free fire-zone. There could have been dozens of such firing positions which were impossible to detect unless they stumbled directly into them.

Deringhouse had only one mutant in his group: Son Okura. The slightly built Japanese with the large horn-rimmed glasses had the unique capability of being able to perceive with his eyes a much wider range of the electromagnetic spectrum than ordinary people. Son Okura was able to see long-wave infra-red as clearly as the shining blue sky on Earth. He was even in a position to receive ultra-violet light and to diagnose it up to a degree.

This came in especially handy at this time because Deringhouse was reluctant to make use of his ultra-lightbeams in spite of the falling darkness for fear that they might be detected by the enemy's instruments. However, as the broiling heat of the day was retained under the dense cover of the jungle, Okura's eyes still performed perfectly. As far as he was concerned the dark night was as bright as a sunlit landscape.

In addition Deringhouse was aided by the small microwave detectors carried on each of the transport vehicles. One of the men was busy combing the surroundings of their landing place. Tiny green points glimmered faintly on the fluorescent screen when the detector beam registered the metallic mass of another rocket ramp.

A second man marked the results of the search on a preliminary map.

As Deringhouse was waiting for the final results the man with a Geiger counter reported unusually high radioactivity. Deringhouse took two men along and a small Geiger counter to track down the source of the radiation. One of the two men was Son Okura.

They approached the incinerated strip.

Okura suddenly stood still and raised his hand. Deringhouse stopped behind him. From the left came a crashing trampling noise. Deringhouse saw a flat long shadow which moved through the thicket about 60 feet ahead of them.

It disappeared again in the jungle in a northern direction and either did not notice the breathlessly waiting three man group or was not interested in them.

They kept marching on, surmounting major obstacles by utilizing the antigrav generators in their transport suits, and reached a spot where the Geiger counter indicated such an intensity that Deringhouse did not dare proceed any farther.

About 300 feet ahead of them – in the section of the jungle which had been flattened by the *Stardust* juggernaut – Okura made out a collection of dark mounds which he guessed to be ruins of buildings. There was no doubt that the radiation emanated from there. Deringhouse was fairly well satisfied that the intruders had stored a part of their arsenal of nuclear weapons in those buildings and that they had gone up in the flames of the holocaust.

He wanted to return but at this moment Okura put a warning hand on his arm.

'Shhhhh!'

They listened. From the southeast rang high hammering blows through the wind raised by the heat from the burned soil. Deringhouse was unable to recognize the noise but Okura knew what it was. 'A machete,' he whispered. 'Somebody is coming; I can see him.'

Deringhouse decided to wait.

The high clapping whacks ceased when the lone man reached the edge of the stripped terrain where he was able to move without hindrance. Neither Deringhouse nor the corporal who accompanied him were able to see him; only the Japanese perceived what was going on. 'A soldier in uniform,' he whispered again. 'He carries an automatic carbine in his left hand and a little instrument in his right.'

A minute later he added: 'He's coming straight toward us. We better take cover.'

They crouched behind the stump of a huge tree which had been swept away and crunched by the storm. Deringhouse held his impulse beamer at the ready.

A little later he saw the shadow of the soldier emerge from the darkness. He could hear the man mumble.

He stood still about 15 feet from their hiding place, carelessly holding the carbine in his left hand. But now he had raised the little box close to his eyes and Deringhouse saw a weak shine which was in his opinion a light-scale.

A Geiger counter. Their adversaries were surveying the dangerous contamination of radioactivity.

Deringhouse did not have much time to think about the best tactic. If he had used his impulse-beamer he would have killed the man, but he preferred to get some information.

Cautiously he raised himself up from behind his cover. The stranger's back was halfway turned toward him. Deringhouse leaped across the short distance with his long legs and before the man knew what happened, he was hit over the head with the butt of Deringhouse's weapon.

His knees buckled and he fell limply to the ground.

'Come over here!' Deringhouse called without raising his voice. 'I've got him!'

*

Maj. Lysenkov was careful not to let his men notice anything but he could no longer keep it a secret from himself. If this uncertainty should last more than a few hours, he would be sure to suffer a nervous collapse.

Before him on the compacted floor of the primitive hut – none of the tents were saved – lay a rough map of the area where Gen. Tomisenkov's military force had landed. According to the best estimates he and his men had arrived at, Lysenkov had marked the map with the line of the withered strip and the point of excessive radio-activity where the war missiles had melted.

As chance would have it, the hot dividing path was at its narowest point in this location. He planned to take the risk and make his men run across the center-line at this spot in another three hours. In their pre-dicament it was not of prime importance that every man get across as long as he, the leader of the group, was fast enough to remain unscathed.

But there was this contaminated patch. If the atomic fallout did not sink rapidly enough to a toler-able level, they would have to wait until the hot lane had cooled off sufficiently at another, wider place. Even Maj. Lysenkov was not immune from atomic radiation.

He had sent out a man to check the fallout.

Lysenkov looked at his watch. What was the matter with that slowpoke?

The major got up and left his hut. He walked in the direction from which the scout had to return. He treaded his way between the dense hanging vines and listened.

Steps.

Lysenkov stopped. The thicket in front of him be-ban to move and a shadow loomed up.

'Where have you been all this time?' Lysenkov snarled at the figure.

The man stood still and gave no answer.

'Come here!' Lysenkov ordered.

The man took a few steps toward him.

'Why were you so long?' Lysenkov repeated. 'Answer me!'

At the moment he finally became suspicious, because the man standing before him was so much smaller than the one he had dispatched, it was already too late.

Leaping like a jungle cat, Okura was at the major's throat. A solid blow with the butt of his impulsebeamer finished the fight before it had begun.

Okura sounded a high-pitched whistle and half a minute later Deringhouse and the corporal joined him.

The Japanese pointed to Lysenkov's motionless body. 'Seems to be the boss,' he whispered.

Deringhouse nodded. 'Tie him up and gag him!' he ordered. 'We'll leave the man here for now.'

Son Okura walked ahead of them. On the path Lysenkov had taken into the jungle, they came upon the little lean-to. In a radius of about 150 feet, Okura made out three more, somewhat larger huts under the trees of the forest. Deringhouse estimated the number of occupants in the crude shelters at about 30 people.

He called in the rest of his group and explained

precisely where to land. The radioactive source was a very convenient reference point.

Eight minutes later the vehicles set noiselessly down on a little spot not far from Lysenkov's hut where the brush had been cleared.

Deringhouse gave brief instructions. Before he had finished, a dark silhouette appeared in front of the hut. Deringhouse looked up in surprise.

'Kto tam?' the man inquired.

The sound of the foreign language made Deringhouse react in a flash. Before the guard realized whether or not the suspicion which had brought him over was justified, Deringhouse had shot him with his impulse-beamer. The thermo-shock acted so fast that the soldier did not even have a chance to scream.

The rest was simple. Single guards were posted before each of the huts. They were quickly overwhelmed with a minimum of noise. The sleepy soldiers inside the huts were unable to offer any resistance. The entire action took no longer than 15 minutes and Deringhouse had made 27 more prisoners, one of whom told him that there were no others left on this side of the divider. Deringhouse dispatched two of his detachment to bring in the soldier they had captured first and who had given them the information about his present position.

A storm began to rage over the jungle as Deringhouse continued his interrogation. However, it took an hour and the storm was calming down again before he learned the full extent of his catch. The tornado produced by the *Stardust* had demolished the greatest part of their atomic weapons and Deringhouse's crew had seized the last five atomic rockets so that the enemy was only left in possession of nuclear weapons with less explosive force than one megaton of TNT. Such armament was presumably as defense on board the few spaceships which had been saved by Tomisenkov, whose name had meanwhile become familiar to Deringhouse.

The worst danger had thus been eliminated.

Deringhouse immediately gave his report on the results of his investigation by hyper-wave radio to Rhodan.

CHAPTER FIVE

THE HOUR OF THE HURRICANE

Whereas Deringhouse and his companions had suffered no ill effects from the passing storm, it had brought severe distress to Tomisenkov and his column which he had joined again with his aide.

Fifteen minutes after the horrible mishap in the lake the third officer in Tomisenkov's retinue had become a casualty when he tried to push a thick and stubborn liana out of his general's way and noticed too late that he had tangled with a snake.

The snake with the dimensions of a boa constrictor escaped quickly across the shoulders of the young officer who had slashed it with his machete, and disappeared in the jungle. To all appearances it had ended well and the officer seemed to be none the worse except for the fright which had shaken Tomisenkov and his aide almost as much as him.

However, a few minutes later the young man suddenly collapsed. Tomisenkov came to his assistance. His neck, the only spot which had been touched by the snake, was swollen so badly that it was larger than the circumference of his head.

Another few seconds and the man was dead.

The aide took the machete out of his hand and continued hacking out a passage. In this manner they moved forward about a mile an hour.

At sunset they noticed that the path cleared by the troop marching ahead of them became less over-grown and the tracks looked more recent. Indeed they caught up in 45 minutes with a group of five lightly wounded men carrying two litters with dis-abled comrades.

Almost at the same time the aide, who carried his radio on a strap around his neck, received a call from another group marching ahead of them that they had found a suitable camping ground in unobstructed ter-rain. Tomisenkov did not hesitate for a moment to leave behind the little group they had just met, although the litter bearers could have used a little well-deserved help with their heavy load. He was anxious to reach the camp before complete darkness set in and hurried forward as fast as he could.

'We'll break the path for you,' he consoled his wounded soldiers.

Shortly after sundown they came to the foot of a rocky mesa from where they had received the mes-sage of the vanguard.

It did not take them long to reach the camp which had been pitched by the soldiers who had arrived before them.

The camp was located within a 100-foot clearing on flat land with low brushes.

Close by was a spring with water running in a little creek down the gentle slope. The water was fresh and potable with an unmistakable high iron content. They took advantage of the opportunity to administer medical treatment to the serious cases whose conditions were aggravated by the difficult transport and the muggy heat . . .

Then the storm broke out.

In the preparatory stage of his expedition Tomisenkov had been advised that due to the extremely slow rotation of Venus great differences of temperature would occur between the day and night phases of the planet giving rise to unusually strong atmospheric disturbances at sunrise and at sundown.

But 'unusually strong atmospheric disturbances' did not convey an adequate concept to Tomisenkov and he, therefore, ignored the warning and simply decided to wait and see what took place.

Had he been told that dusk and dawn would be ushered in with hurricanes, he would have exercised more caution.

When the first howling of the storm commenced from the easterly direction he was only mildly apprehensive and did not let it show when he became more concerned.

When they fully comprehended that the howling presaged an acute threat, it was too late for preventive countermeasures.

The hurricane struck the camp with a giant fist.

For a second time in the day Tomisenkov felt as though gripped by a cruel hand and catapulted into the air. He was flung into a patch of nettles – or what must have been something similar to the stinging variety on earth, since his face and hands soon started to burn painfully. He felt like crying, but, being a tough man, especially with himself, he did not give in.

The storm raged on above him, ripping out the bushes and making it impossible to breathe as long as he faced in the direction of the wind. He turned around and pressed his body hard against the rocky ground.

He was lying there for a few minutes, which seemed like hours, until his eyes got used to the darkness.

He saw something crawling out from under the bushes. The glittering, tough-skinned mass of insects looked like something akin to ants, only each of them was two inches long.

Hundreds were crawling along the ground toward him. Paralyzed by fright, he waited till the first one reached his outstretched hand. The insect reacted to the foreign substance, lowered its head and took a bite. Tomisenkov screamed in pain, pulled back his hand and shook it until the ant fell off. A small blood-red spot remained on the back of his hand.

The incident seemed to have aroused the ants. They quickened their pace and came to attack him.

Seized by panic he jumped up. He had forgotten

about the storm which, however, took a hold of him with irresistible force, lifted him out of the bushes and swirled him around like a leaf. Far to the west, the gust suddenly released its grip and dropped him down. The impact of the fall knocked Tomisenkov out cold.

*

Rhodan and his cadre spent the hour of the hurricane at dusk on safe ground in the jungle. Rhodan knew from his prior visit to Venus that the high wall of trees offered the best protection in the forest. The jungle was so dense and the growth so flexible and resilient that the gales were felt only as an annoying noise in Rhodan's provisory camp.

The camp was situated at the foot of a peculiar stony slope rising gently toward the south and covered with low brush.

Rhodan intended to resume his advance at the end of the storm and to attack the vanguard of the enemy at the earliest opportunity. But he had not the slightest inkling that Tomisenkov himself – whose name he knew from Deringhouse's report – was at this moment no more than a mile and a half away from him on the other side of the ridge formed by the rock 500 feet above the plain of the jungle.

All was quiet on board the *Stardust*.

*

No matter how much the tornado had battered

the camp and its occupants, when everything was over the discipline of the men had been maintained and they knew that it was their first duty to rescue Gen. Tomisenkov.

All the aide could tell them was that Tomisenkov had been swept away toward the west.

Taking torches along, the search party entered the brush. They ran into a swarm of oversize, light-brown ants and had sense enough to make a wide detour around them.

After an hour, they finally found Tomisenkov. He woke up and started cursing volubly. His rib, which had been fractured by the cyclone in the wake of the *Stardust*, must have been completely broken in the last plunge.

The men had to carry Tomisenkov for a while. When he had recovered sufficient strength he continued, with much grunting, under his own power, as he considered the other mode of transport beneath his dignity.

Two of the uninjured men who had remained in the camp had meanwhile taken stock and what they found was highly alarming. The troop had consisted of 30 members – 12 lightly and 18 severely wounded men. Of the latter, six had died and another six could not be found at all. The slightly wounded had suffered two dead and four had disappeared.

The huts had to be reconstructed. Tomisenkov told his aide to radio the spaceships which had landed in the mountains. After a few futile attempts he succeeded in making the connection and Tomisenkov instructed one of the ships to leave again and pick him up. Nothing was left of his resolve to lead the men of his troop as a shining example.

Since the men had been trained under the special conditions prevalent in the jungles of Venus, it took them only 15 minutes to erect a fairly comfortable shelter with a curtain of tightly woven vines on which Tomisenkov had insisted. He knew better than anyone that it would take several hours to get the rocket ready for the take-off and that he would have at least eight hours to recuperate before the pilot could arrive.

He made himself comfortable on a bed of leaves and got involved in a discussion with his aide about the prospects of their enterprise. The pain from his broken rib became more tolerable and his confidence gradually returned after the horrors of the past hours.

In contrast, the aide was pessimistic.

'In my opinion we're fighting a lost cause. It has become clear during the storm that we are utterly unprepared for the vicissitudes of nature on this planet and now we're up against a superior adversary when we can't even cope with the hostile environment of Venus.'

Tomisenkov became angry.

'You can't blame the Fleet Ministry for Rhodan's

presence. They were all convinced that Rhodan was occupied somewhere far out in space. Nobody could reasonably be expected to foresee that he would show up just at the wrong time.'

The aide shrugged his shoulders and prudently chose not to contradict his superior any further.

'What do you think about . . .' Tomisenkov began after a pause, but at this moment the curtain of vines started to move. 'Who is it?' Tomisenkov bellowed.

They heard a gurgling noise outside.

'Take a look!' Tomisenkov ordered his aide.

The officer got up, pulled the curtain aside and stared into two fiery-red glowing eyes close to his face.

He flinched back with a shrill cry but whoever was out there was not fooling around. Tomisenkov, who had watched everything closely, saw a big claw with several toes surge through the curtain and grab his aide by the neck. The victim was dragged outside screaming at the top of his voice and the curtain was torn out with him. Outside the hut was a clumsy, weaving shadow and two fiery red eyes as big as saucers were dancing through the air.

The shouting of the unfortunate prey, taken so gruesomely by surprise, faded away. Tomisenkov, who was scared stiff, heard tramping noises which trailed quickly off in the distance, and finally a peculiar smacking sound.

Then he regained his wits. Disregarding his

aching rib he jumped up from his bed of leaves and yelled:

'Alarm! Help!'

He was heard immediately; but it took a little longer till the summoned men could make sense out of his weird tale. They combed the entire camp ground using the last three electric searchlights left from their equipment. Nothing could be found of the aide nor the mysterious beast to which he had fallen victim. The ground in front of Tomisenkov's shed was fairly hard and there were no tracks visible.

Tomisenkov doubled the guards. He was still busy ordering precautions when a new wild scream came from the back of the camp. The searchlight was swung around at once and revealed a bizarre and terrifying sight where the last unfinished shed stood.

An animal which evidently moved on two legs and at first glance seemed to be almost as large as a house, had pounced onto one of the disabled men and snapped him up in its long, pointed beak. As it was about to carry off its prey, the bright searchlight startled the beast. It closed the big red eyes in its bird-like head and remained in a fixed position as if blinded. The wounded man kept on screaming.

'What are you waiting for?' Tomisenkov hollered. 'Shoot! Shoot it!'

The order goaded the soldiers into action. A volley of shots thundered out, the harsh rattling sounds of the carbines intermingling with the sharp metallic crack of the pistols.

They could clearly see in the light of the beam that many of the bullets had hit their target. The leathery skin of the animal burst open and some kind of blood poured from the wounds. The injured man was suddenly quiet.

The beast appeared to have lost interest in him. It let him drop to the ground and beat a hasty retreat. As it was running away its legs seemed to get longer and Tomisenkov heard for a second time the rapid tramping noise as its feet hit the ground.

The strange creature had been running a distance of 300 feet with steadily increasing speed, when it suddenly unfolded flaps of skin from its back, which spread out to an enormous span of wings. Its starting speed was sufficient to make it soar aloft within a second. It flapped its wings with an unpleasant smacking noise and flew away faster than the searchlights could follow it.

Tomisenkov and his companions were so stunned by the frightful surprise that they hardly dared breathe. After a minute or two one of them said in awe: 'A flying reptile!' His words broke the spell.

They went to help their savagely assailed comrade but he was dead.

Tomisenkov was afraid to return to his hut. He stopped the construction of all huts and told his men to sleep in the open. More than half his men were posted as guards and Tomisenkov cursed the pilot and his outmoded rocket that took so long to get to them.

CHAPTER SIX

... AND AFTER

Rhodan had slept two hours. It was enough to make him feel refreshed.

Consulting the latest observation reports from the *Stardust*, he developed a tentative route on which he figured he would encounter at least two of the opposing detachments.

Before he had finished his work, one of the observers announced: 'Flying object approaching, sir! Size of an airplane but silent.'

Rhodan ran over to the little range finder set and looked in puzzlement at the green spot which slowly wandered to the center of the screen.

'Velocity about 50 miles per hour,' the observer added.

The spot was still some distance away from the center of the screen when it suddenly changed its course.

'He's descending,' the astounded observer said.

Rhodan followed the image with concentrated eyes. He tried to find out what the object was; but other than its size the picture of the microwave screen reflected little else.

The change in altitude had brought the green spot pretty close to the center of the observation screen. However, just before it reached there, it stopped suddenly.

'What have we got here?'

Rhodan now realized that an animal had caused the reflex on the range finder. A rather big creature with wings, possibly a flying reptile. It probably perched somewhere on the trees in the vicinity. The green spot was exactly at the same height as the forest.

'Don't worry,' Rhodan explained to the observer. 'It was probably only an animal. Perhaps a . . .' He stopped in the middle of his sentence. 'Did you hear anything?' he asked.

'I think I did . . .' the other man replied.

They held their breath and listened excitedly.

Before long they heard the sound again. It was a cry uttered in extreme anguish. A human cry.

Rhodan acted without delay. 'Locate direction!' he called to the observer. With that he disappeared into the darkness.

A few seconds later he was ready to start in a transporter with five men. He steered the vehicle over the head of the observer who gave him the exact direction. Then he went up through the cover of the trees and began his search.

The transporter was equipped with its own detection set. On the oscillating screen the colossal beast clearly stood out as a glittering point against the dark background of the forest.

'Have your weapons ready!' Rhodan ordered as he roughly shifted forward on his flight. 'And keep your eyes open. A human life is at stake!'

The distance from his camp to the animal was no more than 200 yards. When the craft had come within 100 feet, Rhodan's group had the target in perfect range. Rhodan switched on the infra-red searchlight and studied the behemoth through the filter. It sat on a gigantic tree and the ugly sight of his bald skin made him shudder.

It was without doubt a flying reptile but it also resembled a bird.

The infra-red beam seemed to bother the animal. It jerked its head up and Rhodan could see the six-foot-long sharp beak.

'Neutron beam!' Rhodan called out without taking his eyes off the filter. 'One hundredth!'

The weak energy emission of the neutron beam was just enough to let the beast feel a lurking danger. It spread its wings and with a smacking sound, which was transmitted by the microphone, rose a few feet above the tree. They could see no sign of the man whose pitiful screams they had heard earlier.

'One tenth!' Rhodan ordered.

The intensity of the neutron beam increased. The creature shrieked and tried to fly away.

'Impulse beamer!' Rhodan shouted.

The terrible weapon blasted the reptile out of the air and it tumbled down into the jungle.

Rhodan started up again. The foliage of the trees was firm enough to hold the transporter aloft. Rhodan set the vehicle down and warned his men to exercise caution as they climbed out.

Once outside the small airlock, they smelled the disgusting stench of the animal's burned body. They climbed down the heavy branches, which had been stripped of leaves by the claws of the beast, and, shining their flashlights, they found the limp body of the man who had cried for help in a forked branch of the tree.

Rhodan examined the man before they lifted him into the transporter. His uniform was torn and he was bleeding from several wounds. Rhodan applied some coagulating remedy from the Arkonide medical supplies on board the *Stardust*.

He did not know the man but judging from his uniform he was a member of the military forces from the Eastern Bloc. If he could keep him alive, he should be able to furnish valuable information.

After they had carefully carried him into the transporter they flew back to their camp.

Responding to the medical treatment which was available there, the man quickly regained consciousness. Rhodan made sure that he did not feel any pain when he woke up. He raised himself up on his elbow and inquired in Russian: 'Where am I?'

'I can't understand you,' Rhodan answered. 'Do you speak English?'

The man nodded. 'Are you . . . Rhodan?' he asked hesitantly.

Rhodan confirmed with a nod. 'And who are you?'

It could very well be that the man had no intention of answering Rhodan's question truthfully. Notwithstanding the fact that Rhodan had saved his life from the clutches of the reptile, he still was his opponent.

But Rhodan's mind had been honed to the finest degree by the treatment he had undergone on the planet Wanderer so that he posed his question with the power of suggestion. The man had no choice but to tell the truth.

'My name is Trevuchin. I'm Gen. Tomisenkov's aide.'

Rhodan was satisfied.

He continued interrogating Trevuchin, who responded with facts and figures in spite of his determination to lead Rhodan thoroughly astray.

*

Tomisenkov did not get a chance to sleep.

His rib ached and the events of the last day were too dreadful to take, even for a man of his fortitude.

When he managed to doze off, fire-spitting hot-eyed reptiles swooped down from the air clamping their long beaks around his neck and shrieking so loudly that he woke up in a sweat.

He rolled around on his other side and stared into the bushes which were set off black against the muddy gray of the sky.

It's the dense atmosphere and the vicinity of the sun, he reflected in his tired state. It never gets completely light on Venus because the air is too dense. Neither can it be perfectly dark as the air is such a good conductor of light.

One of their searchlights kept slowly rotating in a circle from north to east, then south. Tomisenkov closed his eyes to avoid getting blinded when the cone of light passed across the bushes.

When he opened his eyes again he saw that something was moving in the brush. A bulky object emerged.

Tomisenkov was the only one who had noticed it in the light of the beam. At first he thought it was another signal but then he heard the slight humming of a machine.

Perry Rhodan!

The thought struck him like an electric shock.

Rhodan had discovered the location of his camp and had come to attack!

Tomisenkov did not wait to verify his suspicion. Moaning softly, he slowly got up, trying not to attract any attention.

The borderline of the bushes was more than 100 yards away. Rhodan was certain to proceed warily and slowly and by that time he would be safely gone.

It would have been foolish to attempt any resistance to Rhodan with his few sleepy and demoralized defenders. If Rhodan moved against the camp he probably was adequately prepared.

Under the circumstances it was most important that he, Tomisenkov, did not fall into the enemy's hands.

He fled northwest into the bushes, crawled another 50 yards and waited.

Now he took time out to consider his next move. Alone, he had an excellent chance to escape furtively during the turmoil of the battle which was momentarily about to break out.

But when five minutes went silently by without a stir in the camp, he became nervous. The way he figured, Rhodan should already have commenced his attack.

After waiting a few more minutes his curiosity gained the better of him and he cautiously crawled back to the camp.

When he was within earshot he heard voices in the clearing. Getting a little closer he could understand the words spoken in English.

He froze as he listened to Rhodan's instructions to his men:

'He must be hiding somewhere in these bushes. He can't be very far. Go look for him, but watch yourselves!'

The sound of breaking twigs set Tomisenkov in

motion again. He fled once more as fast as he could in the same northwesterly direction.

He felt anything but well as he broke in great haste through the undergrowth in the dark and he did not stop to speculate where his flight would take him. The general direction was correct and perhaps he could somehow draw the attention of the rocket-ship.

What irritated him most was the realization that Rhodan had taken over the camp without a fight. He was silent, cool and efficient.

After a while – he did not know how much time had passed – the terrain which heretofore had been gently rising north, became level and then declined evenly in the same direction.

The brush became denser and gradually a few trees appeared here and there. Whenever he stopped to catch his breath, he could hear the rustling of the leaves and the voices of his pursuers following not far behind.

It was easy enough for them to see his tracks with their lamps.

From now on he proceeded more stealthily. He tried to break fewer twigs and to leave no footprints on the ground.

He was so engrossed in his endeavor that he failed to notice the approaching creature despite its for-midable size and he almost ran into its broad hairy chest when it hissed its foul breath down in his face.

Tomisenkov reacted instinctively, which saved

him. He did not know what kind of an animal it was into whose fangs he had almost blundered. It resembled a bear as much as he could see in the darkness but it was at least three times as big as any bear Tomisenkov had ever seen.

In any case the general leaped frantically to the side and escaped the first strike of its paws. He nimbly jumped a second time and was out of reach of the fearsome animal.

He scrambled away without caring in which direction he moved. He heard the rumbling and stomping noise behind him and looking back over his shoulder he saw the dark swaying mass come after him.

He would probably have been lost if Lady Luck had not come to the rescue.

When Tomisenkov landed after a wide leap across a fallen tree, the ground gave way under his feet. With a muffled cry he stretched out his arms to both sides and tried to grab a hold. However, the treacherous hole exceeded the span of his arms. With nothing to hold him back, he slid down a shaft which was even darker than the night of the jungle.

He plummeted down to a depth of about 20 feet where the shaft took a turn and after a scraping ride he was dumped into a room which – as he soon found out – was formed like a funnel in a fairly regular shape.

He listened closely and heard a deep growl. Clods of dirt poured down the shaft. After a few seconds it was quiet again. Then he heard the bear trotting away.

Tomisenkov took a deep breath. Whatever the quandary in which he found himself, this hole had saved him from the bear.

He struck a match and surveyed his surroundings.

It was a miracle that he was unscathed by the fall. The funnel was about 12 feet high and the hole through which he had entered was about 10 feet above the point of the funnel, a little below the ceiling of the odd room. There were several such openings where other shafts presumably ended.

Unfortunately the wall of the funnel was too steep and too smooth to let Tomisenkov climb up to one of the holes.

He pulled out his knife and went to work cutting steps in the glazed surface of the wall. Though it was difficult, his rate of progress gave Tomisenkov hope that he could cut enough steps to reach a hole in five hours.

For the time being it was essential that Rhodan's men be prevented from capturing him. Down here he felt safe.

Only then did he begin to wonder about the function of the funnel and its inlets. He had noticed that the tip of the cone was filled with waste two feet high. One would have assumed that only dust could have passed through the entrance on the ground since it was closed with a thin cover of soil. But Tomisenkov felt solid objects under his feet.

He lit another match and examined the floor on which he stood. He picked up one of the hard objects to take a closer look.

It was a piece of bone; there could be no doubt about that.

Tomisenkov felt a little perturbed. How did the bone get into this hole?

It was unlikely that rain could have washed out the funnel in such even shape. What about the glaze on the wall and the entrance which was so adroitly camouflaged?

It had to be a trap!

A trap laid by one of those obnoxious beasts which abounded on Venus. Surely, it would come every so often and devour what had been caught in its trap!

Tomisenkov continued his hard work on the wall at top speed under the pressure of growing panic.

*

Perry Rhodan had learned the location of Tomisenkov's camp from his aide and attacked it by means of a psycho-beamer.

The beam covered the entire camp a few seconds after Tomisenkov disappeared; it imposed Rhodan's will on the defenders. They did not object in the least that their arms were taken away and obediently let themselves be tied up with ropes. Nobody offered resistance.

After they had all been safely secured, Rhodan terminated the hypnotic spell and the prisoners began to swear vociferously.

Rhodan did not interfere. He picked out one of them and questioned him about Gen. Tomisenkov who was obviously not among the bunch of soldiers they had overpowered. The man had been standing guard near the bushes where Tomisenkov disappeared and willingly gave information as Rhodan put the full suggestive power of his mind into his question.

Thereupon Rhodan sent a search party after Tomisenkov which was on his heels when he evaded it.

The search party returned after one hour with empty hands. They had found the tracks of a large animal which overlapped Tomisenkov's footprints. That was all. Nobody knew where Tomisenkov had gone.

Another success fell into Rhodan's lap when two hours after seizing the compound an unwieldy rocketship with fiery exhaust landed with laborious maneuvers about half a mile from the camp.

The pilot was taken prisoner as well as the whole crew of the rocketship. They gathered from the pilot that the entire division had no more than 80 operable spaceships left.

Whereupon Rhodan dryly remarked:

'And now there are only 79!'

CHAPTER SEVEN

FUGITIVE ON VENUS

Rhodan assumed that Tomisenkov's fate was sealed. He was convinced that the fugitive had doomed himself senselessly. The people from the Eastern Bloc were so inadequately armed against the perilous conditions existing on Venus that none of their men could hope to stay alive by himself in the jungle for more than half a day.

Rhodan's next target was the new base of the space landing division in the mountains northwest. Judging from the information he had received from the prisoners, he could not expect it to be a pushover. Although Tomisenkov did not know the territory, he had given orders to spread out the remnant of the division over a large area. In view of the inaccessibility of the sprawling terrain, Rhodan had to be prepared to conduct a regular guerrilla war.

It would have been a waste of energy to deploy the weapons of the *Stardust* to attack the mountain camp. The armament of the battleship was intended for compact targets and Rhodan would have to vaporize the whole mountain to make sure that the forces of the Eastern Bloc were completely annihilated.

However he did not have any such thing in mind. His smaller arms far outclassed those of the expeditionary force. If he proceeded with circumspection, he should be able to gain his objective without suffering casualties and without creating major upheavals on the surface of Venus by the indiscriminate use of the *Stardust*'s awesome might.

Obviously, Rhodan had decided to revise his strategy.

He considered it no longer necessary to destroy the invaders. On the contrary, he would have liked it much better if the life of as many as possible members of their division could be spared in the imminent showdown.

Their spaceships had to be destroyed as well as all of their weapons which would create havoc on Venus, but he did not want to kill anyone.

Rhodan had devised certain concrete plans for the future of the other army.

*

Tomisenkov worked so furiously that he did not hear the slithering sound at first.

He stopped what he was doing and became almost stupefied listening to the ominous sound which came closer and closer until something swished through the air.

He did not hazard a guess what it might be. It was pitch dark and he was afraid to light a match.

The terrifying object exuded a stench which nauseated him.

He heard a second swishing noise and felt a strong blow against his shoulder that nearly knocked him down. He noticed, even in his state of fear, that his shoulder had been hit by something rather soft which seemed to be about the size of a big arm.

At least that was how the blow felt.

He ducked and crouched down. He began to see dancing spots before his eyes and was overcome by fright. His forehead broke out in a sweat and his ears were ringing.

He drew his pistol, gathered his last ounce of courage and waited.

The thing he had heard had evidently entered through one of the chutes. The fact that it had not fallen in as he had but apparently approached it slowly, indicated that it was not one of the victims for which the trap was built. It probably was the builder of the pit.

At the moment the animal seemed to be very agitated. Somewhere above Tomisenkov's head it slid around in the darkness and then the soft but powerful arm came down for the third time.

This time it moved purposefully. It crept around Tomisenkov's shoulder and pried under his arms. Tomisenkov forced himself to wait.

When the slimy arm began to lift him up, he fired his pistol.

The shots crashed like roaring thunder in the subterranean room. Tomisenkov felt half unconsciously that the sensitivity of his ears were impaired and he noticed a loud ringing sensation.

The explosions of the shot almost dazed him. He kept his finger on the trigger of the automatic pistol until the firing pin clicked on the empty clip.

The arm which had seized Tomisenkov seemed to tremble. Tomisenkov could feel its grip weaken and he sank to the floor. Eventually the arm let go of him. Wounded by his shots, the ghastly animal above him raised a savage din.

Tomisenkov had his second clip ready to shoot. He thought that he had finished off the beast or that it would get out in a hurry.

Therefore it came as a deadly shock to him when he heard the whooshing sound once again as tentacles slammed down, almost touching his face. When he fell down he had changed his position and the predator had to hunt for him as before.

His nerves were about to give out. He did not want to find out whether the injured animal would manage to grab him a second time. He aimed his pistol in the direction from which the noise came and pulled the trigger again.

When he had emptied the magazine he toppled over and fell face down into the stinking dregs which were collected at the bottom of the funnel.

All his strength had left him. He tried in vain to

raise himself up on his hands but the muscles of his arms were too weak to support his body. Moaning helplessly, he fell over again.

Now he became aware that all was quiet around him.

He listened anxiously.

Other than a slight slithering noise in the distance he heard nothing at all.

His success in driving away the nauseating creature gave him new courage. He finally got back on his feet and after waiting five minutes in complete silence, took a chance and lit another match.

The funnel was as empty as he had seen it half an hour ago. There was no trace of what had happened in the meantime except the holes his bullets had made in the wall.

Tomisenkov was perplexed. There were two distinct rows of bullet holes, one row from each clip he had fired.

The two rows were about equidistant from the opening of one of the shafts leading into the funnel. He had aimed at the shaft opening because he had suspected the animal was there but in the darkness he had hit the wall instead, missing the target equally to the left and to the right.

Each clip contained 50 bullets and – according to Tomisenkov's quick guess – each row of holes apparently consisted of the same number.

Therefore, none of his shots had found its mark.

Why then did his tormenter beat a retreat?

Although this was a very interesting question, the most urgent solution he sought now was how to get out of his trap. With renewed vigor he resumed cutting steps in the wall and soon crawled into the end of the chute through which he had bounced so unexpectedly beneath Venus' surface.

He was afraid he would run into some more difficulties in the shaft but fortunately some growing vines had contributed to the outside cover of the entrance. These vines had been dragged down into the shaft when Tomisenkov tumbled in and now they were hanging there waiting to be used as climbing ropes. Tomisenkov tested their strength, found them satisfactory and clambered up them without delay until he was back on safe ground.

He remained flat on the ground for a while, catching his breath. Then he got up to continue his way in the planned direction.

There was no sign of the pursuers Rhodan had sent after him. In spite of some strange noises around him he got the impression that he was, for the time being, safe from other abominable beasts. In any case he was happy that he was unmolested and that the hunt was over.

Just the same he would have liked to know where the animal into whose trap he had wandered had gone. He had no desire to meet up with it again by fleeing too hastily.

He struck a match and looked around.

The light did not reach very far but he found immediately what he was looking for.

Not the track of the animal but the animal itself.

There was no doubt that it was dead. Had Tomisenkov's olfactory sense been less irritated by the smoke of the powder, he would have noticed the stench sooner.

The creature resembled a mollusk, as he already had deduced, a species of polyps living on land. The main body was about four or five feet high and 10-foot tentacles extended in all directions. One had lifted Tomisenkov up.

Tomisenkov speculated as to why the repulsive organism had died. Finally he concocted a theory which at first glance seemed rather dubious.

His shooting had caused three effects; first the bullet holes themselves, then the powder smoke and fumes and finally the noise of the detonations.

The bullets had evidently missed entirely. This left only the two other effects. Either it must have been poisoned by the fumes or killed by the noise. Tomisenkov could not decide which was the more likely cause of its demise.

He inserted the third clip into his pistol and marched away. The manner in which he had tackled the polyp reinforced his conviction that he would be able to overcome all other challenges of the jungle.

*

By this time Rhodan had gathered all necessary intelligence pertaining to strength, personnel and intentions of the Eastern Bloc units.

He knew that the expedition was originally comprised of 500 spaceships.

Gen. Tomisenkov was in command. Serving under him were two major generals, five colonels and a great number of lower ranking officers. Only one of the major generals was still alive, Lemonovich, and Rhodan's prisoners were certain that he would take over the command of the remaining division as soon as he came to the conclusion that he could not count on Tomisenkov's return.

The objective of the expedition was clear. When Rhodan had returned from his first voyage to Venus he had not kept it a secret that he had made important discoveries on that planet, discoveries of a scope to make him independent of the good or ill will of the various power blocs on Earth.

The Eastern Bloc did not know the details of his discovery. In any case the new government which in the interim had seized power in the Eastern Bloc coveted his base on Venus and attempted to occupy it. This was the purpose for which Tomisenkov's division had been thoroughly trained. It was launched into space in 500 spaceships to land on Venus.

Even more remarkable than the unabashed aggression exhibited by the ambitious government of the Eastern Bloc was the technical excellence with which it had been achieved. The vessels of the space landing division were equipped with nuclear engines of the same type which the first *Stardust* had used on Rhodon's flight to the moon. The trip to Venus took four weeks and the armada had accomplished it without a single loss.

'People of such caliber are capable of conquering the universe,' Rhodan mused bitterly, 'if only they weren't put on the wrong track by some fools.'

Proceeding according to his plan, he flew northwest from the raided camp to rout the remnants of the division from their new hiding places. Meanwhile Deringhouse had rejoined his little troop. He had taken Lysenkov and his men to the *Stardust* where Lysenkov underwent further interrogation under hypnotic influence. Lysenkov's statements were compared with those of Trevuchin, Tomisenkov's aide. There were no discrepancies and none were expected.

At midnight, Venus time, Rhodan's detachment reached the foot of the mountain where the survivors of the expeditionary force had concealed their last spaceships. Rhodan had very little to go by in ferreting out the hostile battleships since the *Stardust* had observed nothing more than the course of their flight. But he knew that they were distributed over an area of 3000 square miles and therefore presumed that the crews would communicate by radio from time to time.

He posted his men on elevated spots and instructed his radio operators to monitor the communications between the members of the opposing division and to pinpoint their locations.

After approximately 80 hours he had already marked 50 different spots on his map – each one representing the location of one of their transmitters.

The points lined up in three, sometimes four rows across the central part of the mountain. While Rhodan was unable to make out any detailed features from the map which he had drawn on his first flight to Venus, he was nevertheless convinced that there were valleys where the points were recorded. It was highly unlikely that the rocketships would have set down on exposed slopes or peaks.

At 85:00 o'clock, when the night neared its end, Rhodan departed with his group. Bell had reported from the *Stardust* that everything was in order. He also emphasized that time was of the essence. The computer on board the *Stardust* had given a warning signal. There was little time left to gain entrance to the Venusian fortress. If too much time elapsed, even the main positronic brain in the fortress would be precluded from computing the complete orbit of the planet Wanderer on the basis of the known fragment of its curve.

The transporters flew along the mountain slopes in the same northwesterly direction. They moved along at an average altitude of 12,000 feet above the plain. But even at this height the mountain slopes were covered by the jungle as densely as the level plain.

A 12,000-foot difference in altitude did not cause any significant change in the hot, moisture-laden climate of Venus.

The observation screens reflected the bizarre surroundings. The mountains were still young and the formations were distinguished by steep and abrupt changes in their contours.

At 88:00 o'clock the aerial flotilla was above the first spot marked on the map. Rhodan did not care to attack at this location simply because it was closest. He preferred to approach from the north in order to throw the enemy into confusion.

One hour later the transporters had reached the center of the row of points on the map. Rhodan veered to the south and closed in on a spot from which he had received one of the strongest signals.

The first light of day appeared over the horizon as Rhodan cautiously steered the craft over the sharp edge of a precipice where a deep basin was gouged out like a vertical cylinder. The floor of the basin was 6000 feet below the edge. The walls of the basin went straight down, exposing many fissures. The diameter of the basin measured about five miles.

The transporters descended close to the mountain wall. The day had not yet dawned inside the valley. It was dark and unless the adversary happened to aim their radar against the mountain walls they would have no warning of the incipient attack.

The spaceship could only be detected on the screen

of the range finder. So far the infra-red searchlight showed nothing and Son Okura was unable to recognize anything either. Apparently the rocketship stood in the midst of very high trees. The gap it had broken when it landed was already covered up by the luxuriant growth of the vegetation on Venus.

Rhodan touched down not far from the wall. He left a complement of four men behind to guard the transporters. He led the others into the jungle toward the spaceship whose position had been fairly well determined by the range finder.

They moved along the floor of the forest. Rhodan thought it would be too risky to make use of their transport suits. This way it took them two hours to reach the neighborhood where their goal was hidden.

By now it was also lighter in the valley. Son Okura was no longer the only one who could see something.

And then they discovered the spaceship.

It had sunk a few yards into the soft ground of the jungle and stood a little askew. Doubtlessly it was still intact and a skilled pilot would not have too much trouble to get the slanting ship off the ground.

It was standing on its rear fins. The outline of an airlock hatch was visible on the metallic skin of the hull between two of the fins. Rhodan motioned his men to stop.

'We'll burn out the hatch,' he suggested. 'It won't take more than a minute. They haven't noticed anything in there as yet. Each of these vessels has quarters where 20 men can be carried. The cockpit is at the top. I don't know how many people are inside but they could be either in the crew deck or in the cabin, so watch out! We don't necessarily want to wring their necks but if there's any resistance we'll shoot. Is that clear? Nothing must go wrong!'

CHAPTER EIGHT

FIVE LEVELS OF PERIL

Maj. Gen. Lemonovich had concealed his rocket near the northwest of the chain. A second ship had landed in the same valley shortly after his own.

Upon receiving Gen. Tomisenkov's call for help, he had ordered one of the ships at the far end of the chain to leave and to pick up the general. After 100 hours had passed and the ship had not reported back, he assumed that it had either crashed or that it was shot down by the enemy. During that time he had not communicated with the general or his aide. He had made every effort to get in touch with them by radio and concluded that they too had fallen victim to the fateful environment.

He had advised his troops that Gen. Tomisenkov had probably lost his life or was in the hands of the enemy and that he as highest ranking officer assumed command of the division.

This had sounded very efficient but after he had made his announcement he racked his brains what to do next.

His hiding place was evidently safe. What he had feared most had not occurred; his opponents had not turned the mountains into a smoldering, radioactive wasteland as they were in a position to do with their advanced weapons, if they chose. He did not know why Rhodan had neglected to do this but he was happy with his stroke of luck.

Nevertheless, they had not come here to while away their time in a hide-out till his ships rotted away and his soldiers got old. Something had to be done.

As the day was breaking, Lemonovich was sipping black coffee, which had been strictly rationed. While pondering his problems, something came up which eliminated his headaches with one stroke.

With a hard knock somebody pushed open the trapdoor hatch, which separated the cockpit from the quarters of the crew below, and stuck his head in. Lemonovich wanted to rebuke him but the highly excited man blurted out: 'News, sir! C-145 was attacked by the enemy. Only five men are still holding out in the pilot's cabin. They're calling for help. Rhodan himself is taking part in the raid!'

Lemonovich was stunned for a few seconds. He was aware of the danger which threatened the C-145 and a moment later realized the opportunity presented to him.

He jumped up to push the button activating the alarm sirens and shouted to the messenger: 'Get me the gunners and their officer right away!'

The trapdoor slammed shut. Lemonovich bent over a large sheets of graph paper on which the position of each of his ships had been noted to a precise degree. The outline of the mountain had merely been roughed in according to vague estimates.

When the officer and his gunners came running through the trapdoor, Lemonovich had already determined the target.

He pulled the officer by his arm to the map. 'Here!' he panted. 'This is the C-145. It has been attacked by Rhodan and his gang. Fire a salvo of at least five missiles at the C-145. We'll never have another chance like this. Shoot at a steep angle! I don't want the missile to get hung up on a mountain peak.'

The officer nodded and gave his men the coordinates which he read from the map. The three non-coms proceeded to set the launchers.

The officer who had complied with Lemonovich's orders suddenly hesitated. 'Is the C-145 already in Rhodan's hands sir?' he asked. 'I mean, have all our men lost their lives?'

But Lemonovich yelled: 'Now we've got a chance to get Rhodan and we're going to get him!'

The young officer shrugged his shoulders.

'Ready to fire!' one of the gunners reported.

And the officer, with a quick glance at Lemonovich, gave the command:

'Fire!'

*

The 40 men in the lower quarters surrendered at

once. However they did not give themselves up without noise and the five men up in the cockpit were alarmed. They bolted the trapdoor and it took four psycho-beamers considerable time to penetrate through the solid metal and to break the opposition of the inmates.

The hatch was opened and Rhodan was in a great hurry to enter the cockpit. The five men stood around the trapdoor and looked as if they had expected Rhodan's visit for a long time.

Rhodan motioned the Japanese to come up. Son Okura scurried up in no time.

'Ask them,' Rhodan ordered, 'whether they have transmitted any radio messages.'

Okura translated the question into Russian. Rhodan saw that one of the men nodded affirmatively. The man said a few words and Okura translated: 'He has informed Maj. Gen. Lemonovich that their ship is under attack and that you are personally leading the offensive.'

Rhodan whirled around and shouted through the hatch: 'Leave ship immediately! Extreme danger!'

There was a great commotion. Only Rhodan's men knew that he meant it when he cried 'extreme danger'. The prisoners were less impressed by the urgency despite the hypnotic influence they were under and their captors had to drive them out with force.

'To the transporters!' Rhodan yelled from behind. He pushed the five men out of the cockpit and down the ladder, following last with Okura. Okura was curious why they were in such a haste but he did not even have time to ask questions.

Once outside the ship Rhodan showed the prisoners the direction in which they had to go.

Son Okura translated: 'Follow the path we've cleared and run like the devil if you value your lives!'

Rhodan and the Japanese ascended in their Arkonide transport suits and moved speedily over the treetops of the forest. They could see the other men down below. Rhodan had no illusions about the prisoners. He knew that – once they were outside the range of the psycho-beamer – they would rally and possibly make a counterattack. He was very anxious to warn them of the peril.

The transporters were ready to start when Rhodan and Okura reached the landing place. They went immediately aboard and rose up along the walls of the crater.

Rhodan finally took time to inform his men about their vulnerable situation. 'Lemonovich, the new commander of the division,' he said over the telecom, 'is aware of our action. He even knows I'm part of it. So we'll have to expect him to try everything in his power – without regard to the safety of his own compatriots – to crush us. As we know the ships of the Eastern Bloc have ... oh, here they come already!'

The transporters had risen about halfway to the

rim of the crater when four blinding explosions flashed one after another down in the valley. A quick eye could see that two of them were right on target over the landing place of the ship while the other two occurred a little farther south.

A tremendous pressure wave shook the transporters in a fraction of a second. Simultaneously the crashing boom of the detonations rolled in, deafening the ears of the men in the vehicles.

The crafts were equipped with automatic stabilization devices. They maintained their balance and utilized the waves of the explosions as uplift, which carried them higher and faster than their engines could have.

They reached safety when they passed over the rim and there set down on the ground.

Rhodan went back to look down into the basin. He knew that he was exposing himself to a risk since the radioactive fallout from this medium-sized defense missile was considerable. His suit – so excellent as a means of propulsion – offered little protection against radiation.

There was no sign of the crew he had chased out of their ship. Rhodan had not expected more than one missile. Now that Lemonovich had fired four of them in his desperate effort to be on the safe side, it was questionable that any survivors were left from the C-145.

Nevertheless, he advised the *Stardust* and gave

instructions to Bell to dispatch another transporter immediately with a crew in radiation-proof outfits to search for anyone still alive.

In the meantime, one of Lt. Tanner's men had observed that a fifth missile had exploded on the flank of a peak which bordered the basin on the west, where it had blown out a big crater.

Rhodan and his detachment of 50 men took off again a few minutes later, partly to escape the area of increasing radioactivity and partly to follow up his first charge as quickly as possible with a second one. Rhodan did not delude himself about the growing difficulties he had to face. Lemonovich had been warned. Unless he was firmly convinced that Rhodan had perished in the bombardment, he was bound to pass on the warning to his officers.

For the time being Rhodan was satisfied that the marauders had one ship less.

The count was down to 78.

*

At 110:00 o'clock local time, Tomisenkov came to a spot in the jungle where he believed he recognized a path beaten by his own men.

He could have been mistaken. The incredible growth of the Venus plants could make any track disappear within an hour. But the new growth consisted mainly of young, thin shoots.

Tomisenkov made a closer inspection and found

91

that he was right. His soldiers must have marched through here and if he followed the trail he could soon be able to join them at the end of his trek.

In the hours that passed – days on the Terrestrial time scale – Tomisenkov had changed greatly.

He had become stooped and his hair had turned white.

He had killed two of the monster bears that wanted to eat him, slain a snake with his hands and shot perhaps 15 more. He had escaped another of the polyps that were also prowling around on land hunting for food in addition to their traps. Climbing up on a tree, he jumped like a monkey through the branches. He moved so fast that the mollusc could not follow him. At the end of his trip through the trees he was caught in a spiderweb of enormous dimensions with threads as thick as his fingers. He was dangerously close to the ugliest spider – much bigger than he – when he finally succeeded in tearing the tough net by setting it into rhythmic motion. He spent the next two hours ridding himself of the sticky threads and until he had regained his freedom of movement he had been utterly defenseless.

At 115:00 o'clock he took a long rest, ate what food he had been able to collect on the way and slept in the forked branches high on a tree.

In the meantime he had learned that life in the jungle varied on four different levels. The lowest was the world of polyp traps and horny creatures living in symbiosis with large white worms. The mean of this level was about 15 feet under ground. The second level was the ground itself with all its ferocious animals, the saurians foremost among them, although Tomisenkov had not yet encountered them. The predatory bears were also a species of saurians, as Tomisenkov later found out, but of a different variety.

The third level was in the treetops of the smaller woods, about 30 feet above the ground. This was the habitat of the spiders of which there were a great deal more present than Tomisenkov first suspected. The reason was that there nets were camouflaged so skillfully that they were difficult to detect if one did not know where to look for them.

The fourth level between 60 and 120 feet was in the higher treetops with less animal life. There were small flying lizards the size of sparrows and pigeons and a few strange but harmless animals which appeared to Tomisenkov to belong to an intermediate stage between lizards and the lowest warm-blooded species. In any case, here it was possible to exist without being eaten up on the spot and Tomisenkov had learned to take advantage of this. At first it bothered him to be waked up from deep sleep by the curious flying lizards that landed on his face but then he got used to the fact that even the most comfortable place on Venus was worse than spending a night in the open on the Siberian taiga.

However he had to be careful to stay away from the uppermost plane of the trees. Above the trees was what might be called the fifth level, the region of the big flying reptiles of the type that had snatched away his aide Trevuchin.

As long as he remained under cover in the foliage, he did not have to be afraid of them.

Around noon Tomisenkov resumed his trek. Five hours sleep had sufficed to refresh him. The jungle was steaming under the hot sun and the ground temperature rose to 120°F. Tomisenkov had gradually become more acclimatized.

He followed the trail which had been broken by his men, pushing the thin newly-grown shoots and vines out of the way with his arms.

After two hours he noticed that the ground began to rise. A few minutes later the grade had become quite steep and the sweat was dripping from Tomisenkov's forehead.

When he came to a gap in the leaves of the trees, he saw the high peaks of the mountains almost vertically above him.

He had reached the mountains! He had made it!

Tomisenkov was confident that he would meet the first of his countrymen before the day was over.

His path, which hitherto had run in a straight line through the jungle, began to twist in curves. Rocks of all sizes were imbedded in the forest and at times it was so steep that Tomisenkov was compelled to advance on all fours.

He became very impatient. He rushed forward and disregarded everything, concentrating on his way in the wild hope that he would run into his people around the next turn.

It wasn't the next turn nor the one after that. It was 10 hours since his last rest when he arrived at a narrow ravine which was the entrance to a deep valley running almost exactly north between the mountain walls. Tomisenkov was very surprised to see that the floor of the valley was nearly bare of vegetation – the first such place he had come across on Venus. Volcanic steam might have been responsible for this uncharacteristic feature, as Tomisenkov noticed plumes of vapors drifting along the walls.

The high mountains enclosing the gorge kept so much of the dim light out of the valley that the visibility was limited to 300 feet. Since it was manifest that his people had entered the valley, Tomisenkov did not hesitate to do the same.

He had left the border of the jungle only a few yards behind him when the air began to change. He smelled sulphur and a few other malodorous scents. Tomisenkov stood still and sniffed a little. It did not seem to be dangerous. It only irritated his throat slightly, that was all.

He went on and after another half hour he wondered how long this valley would stretch, when he was challenged by a voice out of the darkness between some fallen rocks.

The call was in Russian. But Tomisenkov had not heard a human voice in such a long time that he was even startled by his own mother tongue. He dropped to the ground with the alacrity he had learned in the jungle and took cover behind a rock.

'Tomisenkov!' he called back. 'Who's there?'

A derisive laugh came from the dark.

'You'll have to tell that to somebody else! Tomisenkov is dead!'

Tomisenkov was irate and jumped up.

'Look, you fool!' he shouted. 'Am I Tomisenkov or not?'

The guard answered imperturbably.

'First drop your gun and then I'll take a look at you!'

Tomisenkov obeyed.

'Alright. I'm coming.'

The soldier came out from his hiding place with a machinegun in his hands. He stopped six feet from Tomisenkov and scrutinized him. He was baffled by Tomisenkov's white hair and the beard he had grown in the meantime. To boot, the general had not had a chance or had not found it convenient to wash himself. Every square inch of his skin was covered with a crust of dirt.

Nevertheless, the guard recognized him. 'The general . . . !' he gasped in amazement. 'Really!' The guard turned around and pointed his hand into the valley. 'Back there is the C-103. It's the last ship we've left!'

Tomisenkov was taken aback. He could not utter a sound.

'No, that's not quite right,' the sentry corrected himself. 'We've got a few others, but they're down flat, or their fuel tanks have run out, or their reactors are burned up. I don't know what else is the damn matter with them. Whatever it is, the C-103 is the only one which can still get up.'

Tomisenkov did not harbor too many delusions during the absence but this exceeded his worst fears. It took him some time to get over the shock.

'Take me to your post!' he ordered the guard.

CHAPTER NINE

INVISIBLE MEN

Rhodan had proceeded systematically and with dispatch. The attack on the C-145 remained an isolated case. Subsequently Rhodan had directed his men to stake out several places simultaneously and ordered them to take no risks. They used the deflectors of their transport suits and closed in invisibly on the hostile spaceships. They placed explosives under the rear fins of the ships, which were powerful enough to make them topple over. They peppered the fuel tanks so that the precious liquid hydrogen evaporated rapidly or they damaged the drive reactors and incapacitated them permanently.

There were practically no untoward incidents during these actions. At noon there were only three enemy ships left, which Rhodan intended to knock out on his return trip. Two of them were destroyed at 125:00 o'clock and Rhodan prepared to stalk the remaining C-103 with special care because more than 2000 men of their 5000 survivors were posted there.

*

There was a good reason for this.

After the evacuation of their first camp, the great majority of the survivors were forced to march through the jungle and were denied all comfort.

When the troops reached the mountains, they arrived at the C-103, which had landed farthest to the east. Since most of the marchers were disinclined to walk farther than the 120 miles they already had done in order to get to the next ships, they preferred to stop here. Only a few of the toughest and most courageous soldiers and some of the slightly wounded continued on to seek shelter in the more distant ships.

The 2200 men Gen. Tomisenkov found in the camp near the C-103 expected Rhodan's forthcoming attack any moment.

Tomisenkov realized at once that he had to stake everything on one card and he began to organize a reception for Rhodan. Meanwhile he had learned that only very few of the ships overwhelmed by Rhodan had maintained radio contact. They assumed that nobody had escaped death at the other places. However, Tomisenkov corrected this opinion quickly and definitely.

'In all those cases,' he explained, 'where Rhodan put our rockets out of action by bringing them down on their sides, the fall must have demolished the radio transmitters as well and as soon as our technicians have repaired them we'll hear from them again.'

The reports coming in from those ships whose

radio stations had remained intact seemed more than confused to Tomisenkov. All agreed on one point though, namely that nobody had been able to observe the approach of the raiders despite the strictest surveillance in the ships' vicinity.

'Damn it!' Tomisenkov fumed. 'Nobody can make himself invisible!'

Just the same, he was not so certain about it any more.

Even more incredible was the fact that Rhodan – according to the reports received – had inflicted no casualties whatsoever. This probably was not the case where the ships had been overturned. Surely there must have been some dead and wounded but everything in the reports indicated that Rhodan made every effort to conduct his operation in a bloodless manner.

'Why?'

First of all Tomisenkov had two launching ramps removed from their mountings in the C-103 and set up outside with a supply of projectiles. He did not want to be caught short without weapons if Rhodan succeeded in overthrowing his last ship.

The projectiles had a compact shell and contained a non-critical mass of plutonium. It became critical with a thick-walled reflector of beryllium oxide. The ignition worked on the principle of implosion. The missile including its propulsion mechanism was not much larger than the shell of a big cannon.

Next Tomisenkov posted lines of riflemen behind the numerous rocks of all shapes and sizes on both sides of the valley. The signal corps set up lines of communications with the forward guards at both exits of the valley in order to warn Tomisenkov as soon as Rhodan approached.

Moreover, Tomisenkov ordered strict radio silence. There was no doubt that Rhodan had found their positions so quickly because the radio messages from ship to ship had made it easy to home in on them. Tomisenkov was furious when he heard that nobody had even thought of severing the radio communications.

Tomisenkov's last instructions went to the approximately 1500 men who had been assigned no special tasks. They were told to behave as if they felt completely safe. Tomisenkov was certain that Rhodan would observe their camp for a while before he attacked.

*

Rhodan came from the north. It was about 140:00 o'clock when the transporters flew over the entrance to the basin and landed about 3000 feet above the floor of the gorge on the western rim.

From there they surveyed the encampment.

'It looks alright, sir,' Maj. Deringhouse said.

Rhodan peered through his binoculars.

'Some prisoners have claimed that there is a garrison of 2200 soldiers here,' Rhodan pondered. 'There are only about 1500 men down there. Where are the rest?'

Deringhouse shrugged his shoulders. 'I don't know. Maybe they went hunting?'

Rhodan laughed. 'Seven hundred of them? No, my friend, there's something fishy. They know we're coming and they are prepared for us.'

Deringhouse took his field glasses again and studied the valley. As Tomisenkov had concealed his riflemen very well he was unable to detect them.

Maj. Nyssen and Lt. Tanner proposed to forego the established procedure and to destroy the entire camp with the spaceship by dropping an atom bomb on it.

However, Rhodan declined their suggestion. 'I need every man on Venus,' he answered.

He decided to go down with Tanner and Deringhouse to scout the camp. Nyssen was left in charge of the transporters.

Using the deflectors, Rhodan and his companions made themselves invisible. The only thing that remained in sight was the detonator which Tanner carried to be placed under the rear fin of the C-103. It was the size of a melon and a little too big to be entirely confined within the field of the deflector.

The disadvantage of the deflector field was that the wearers of the transport suits were unable to see each other any better than those outside. Rhodan and his two officers had to hold hands during their flight in order to stay together.

*

Lt. Josip was posted in the last line of riflemen close to the wall on the west. He had already spent a few hours guard duty at his post and had meanwhile begun to curse the world in general and Gen. Tomisenkov in particular because he had forbidden smoking.

He wanted a cigarette very badly but could not have one.

Something hit him on the shoulder and smacked to the ground.

A small, rather flat stone.

Josip turned around and tried to find out where the stone had come from.

Obviously from above. Sometimes loose stones fell, making his spot a little hazardous. He was likely to break his neck here, even without Rhodan on the prowl.

Josip reclined again to his former position and aimed his automatic pistol at random out of sheer boredom. From here—

Josip strained his eyes and tapped himself on the head. But the thing was still there.

It looked like a semisphere, dark gray and about six inches in diameter. The semisphere floated in the air, perhaps three, four feet above the surface of the flat rock behind which Josip had stretched out.

It bobbed up and down and retreated slowly.

He carefully raised the barrel of his gun and took aim. At that moment somebody slapped down his arm from behind.

'Cut out this nonsense!' a voice hissed. 'What are you shooting at?'

Josip was startled and spun around. It was Capt. Liubol standing behind him. Josip pointed his trembling hand in the direction of the suspended semisphere and stammered: 'There, look, there is ...' Flabbergasted, he stopped in the middle of his words. The semisphere had vanished.

However Liubol had become curious and Josip told him his story. Liubol's mien was skeptical and he said: 'Come on, if you let me have a swig from your bottle, I'll keep my mouth shut!'

*

Lt. Tanner appraised the situation to determine the most favorable way of bringing down the ship. He decided to place his melon under the rear fin toward the inside of the valley and he did it without anyone noticing him.

The explosion would rip off the fin and make the ship tip over to the inside. The forward end was going to hit the ground not far from the nearest soldiers, whom Tomisenkov had told to sit still and act naturally and unconcerned. They were bound to get a healthy lesson.

'Ready?' Rhodan whispered.

'Yes, sir!' Tanner replied.

He was unable to see Rhodan, but he felt the touch of his hand.

'Careful, get back!'

They retreated the same way they had come. Before reaching the first line of defense, Rhodan gave the order to switch on the antigrav apparatus and fly over the guardsmen instead of wending their way between them as they had done previously.

And then the accident happened.

Deringhouse stood on the slanted surface of a rock. As he turned on the antigrav, he slipped. He did not have time to adjust the neutralizer so that his transport suit would carry him upward. Cursing angrily, he fell on the slab and rolled down the slope till he bumped into the soft ground of the valley.

He had remained invisible all the time but his swearing could be heard and one of the guards saw the impression of Deringhouse's body in the soft soil.

The soldier did not bother to speculate about the evidence and whether such a thing was possible at all – he fired a shot. He shouted to the men around him and pointed with his outstretched arm to the impression of the body. Within seconds the fire from at least 20 automatic pistols concentrated on the hapless major.

Deringhouse's transport suit was equipped with a defense screen from which the bullets recoiled and fell harmlessly to the ground. However, the protective screen was only designed to withstand the fire from one or two such weapons. If the screen had to absorb the continuous bombardment of hundreds of bullets, it required additional energy which could only be drawn, first from the gravity neutralizer and second from the video deflector field projector.

As a consequence Deringhouse not only lost the mobility of his transport suit but his video deflector also ceased to operate, which made him visible again. Moreover, the impact from the pistol shots caused a tremendous vibration which prevented him from simply running away.

With a great effort he managed to get into a position to return the fire with his impulse beamer. Conforming to Rhodan's wishes to spare as many lives as possible, he drew a line of searing heat over the stony barricades behind which the forward guard was posted, forcing the men to keep their heads down and to crawl away as best they could from under the lethal curtain.

However, he did not succeed in gaining his freedom because other troops farther away also rained their withering fire on him.

'Don't give up!' Rhodan called from somewhere and Deringhouse bellowed in agreement.

He knew that Rhodan and Tanner would not leave him in the lurch.

His situation was not overly rosy. He was protected from injuries but the concentrated steady fire prevented his antigrav and video deflector from functioning. He was pinned down out in the open for everyone to see.

*

Gen. Tomisenkov took immediate cognizance of the facts that had transpired. It did not take him more than a second to revise the opinion that his enemy was incapable of making himself invisible.

With lightning speed he summoned his forces from the outlying positions to throw them into the struggle where Deringhouse was fighting desperately for his mobility and invisibility.

At this time Tanner detonated by radio impulse the melon under the rear fin of the battleship. Deringhouse, who was only about 300 feet from the ship, was thrown up into the air and came down farther away. From his new spot he could see the upper end of the rocketship lean over to the side over a huge cloud of dust and disappear underneath. A moment later the ground began to shake from the shock of the metal colossus.

The shooting had been interrupted for a few seconds. Deringhouse's video deflector began to function again and simultaneously he could feel the gentle pull of the antigrav field.

At this time Maj. Nyssen had already committed his unfortunate error. Notwithstanding his limited view of the battle, which took place down in the valley, and convinced that Rhodan and his men were endangered in some inexplicable manner, he had ordered his detachment to go to the rescue. All transporters save one, which was left behind as a reserve on the rim of the mountains, descended into the gorge along the wall.

Rhodan countermanded Nyssen's orders when he saw the transporters coming down but the telecom was so busy with many voices that he did not get through. Besides, he had only realized Nyssen's intentions when the transporters had almost reached the bottom.

The transporters spread terror among the rear lines of the defense. The vehicles landed almost noiselessly. There were excited voices, yet nobody could be seen. Then the boulders began to glow and melt before their terrified eyes.

There was nothing for Tomisenkov's men to do but flee. They deserted their positions and ran in headlong flight into the valley.

Tomisenkov surveyed the debacle and realized that he was almost powerless against such foes.

Almost! But there was still a possibility.

He called three of his officers to the side and hastily gave them instructions. The officers went on their way toward the northern exit of the valley.

Rhodan called for retreat.

At the same time the enemy, who had taken up new positions in the middle of the valley, started to rake the transporters with their fire. As the transporters were enclosed in strong defense screens, they were impervious even to the shelling by mortars. However Rhodan's men became visible when they entered the transporters in the barrage, and they drew the massed fire from the advancing riflemen.

Rhodan made sure that everyone was aboard and then gave the order to start. The machines leaped into the air and ascended along the cliffs.

All transporters – save one.

Deringhouse had retreated a little farther north when the big tumult broke out. When Rhodan called everybody back, he flew toward the transporter which had landed farthest north.

He could hear voices inside the craft. The crew had followed Rhodan's orders. Deringhouse did not pay much attention to the fact that there was no shooting at this transporter in contrast to the fusilades at all the others; but he heard the men grumble as they tried to start the generator.

'What's the matter?' he asked gruffly.

He could not see anyone and nobody could see him.

'The thing won't start!' an invisible speaker complained.

'Let me take a crack at it!'

Deringhouse slipped into the driver's seat. He pushed the green button which switched on the generator and waited for the familiar hum.

Nothing happened.

'We've got no time to lose!' he bellowed. 'Try and find room in one of the other vehicles or use your suits to fly up! Get going!'

The patter of their feet soon faded away.

Deringhouse dropped over the side of the transporter and looked at the chassis from underneath. He saw at first glance the neatly cut oval hole above which the positronic impulse relay had been mounted before; it transmitted the manipulations of the pilot to the propulsion of the craft.

Somebody had taken it out. Somebody who knew next to nothing about the mechanism of the machine. Otherwise he would have removed the generator.

In any case, the loss of the impulse relay was enough to disable the vehicle.

At this moment Deringhouse drew fire. Someone had noticed his footprints on the ground.

The fire was not very heavy. His protective screen reflected it without draining energy from the antigrav or video deflector. Deringhouse got up and saw half an arm and the barrel of an automatic stick out from behind a boulder about 60 feet away. He leveled his impulse beamer at the boulder. It became white hot and Deringhouse figured it was time to clear out.

Meanwhile the transporters had almost reached the rim of the mountains. Deringhouse depended on his transport suit. He put his antigrav into high, lifted himself off the ground and sailed up the cliffs. It took him a little longer than the transporters to reach the top but now that he left no tracks on the ground he was no longer molested.

The sounds of shot died away in the basin since all the targets were gone. The dust raised by the explosion under the C-103 had settled. Deringhouse could see that the rocket had burst wide open. It would never fly again.

Rhodan's men had taken three prisoners who had escaped the fire of their countrymen with slight injuries as they were led to the transporters. Rhodan considered it necessary to interrogate the prisoners as soon as possible, yet he felt that they were not quite out of danger. Therefore, he ordered his column to return home at once.

Deringhouse reported how the last transporter had been prevented from leaving. Rhodan raised his eyebrows and commented with sincere admiration: 'There is a wily fox in charge down there!'

*

Tomisenkov was advised that his casualties amounted to seven dead and 22 seriously wounded men.

However his mind was on something else.

He was in the middle of a conference with the electronic specialists of the C-103.

'Take the part,' Tomisenkov urged them, 'and replace it where it was cut out. This shouldn't be hard to do. Then get the thing going again.'

The electronic technicians went to work. It presented no difficulties to replace the block. Since the cut was in an irregular oval line, there was only one position which matched it.

As the Arkonide technique of impulse transmission did not involve electric wires, there was no problem of how to make connections. The part was put in place, welded in and was ready to function again.

All that was left for the technicians to do was to try out the various buttons and levers and observe how the vehicle reacted.

In less than an hour they had determined exactly how to drive and fly the transporter, how to turn left and right or up and down. Tomisenkov's most urgent demand had been fulfilled.

CHAPTER TEN

CONDEMNED TO VENUS

Rhodan made a temporary stop on the shore of a little lake, situated halfway between the C-103 camp and the *Stardust*, in order to conduct the interrogation of the captives.

He questioned the prisoners himself and thus did not require the application of the psycho-beamer.

When he had learned everything he wanted to know, Rhodan deliberated about the situation with Maj. Deringhouse.

'Tomisenkov has appeared on the scene again,' Rhodan said. 'No one knows how he was able to struggle his way through to the C-103 but he finally did it.'

Deringhouse looked amazed. 'How far is that from their first camp? Wait ... almost 120 miles, isn't it? – 120 miles on foot through the Venus jungle and all he had was an automatic pistol.'

'And he traveled half the way by night,' Rhodan added.

Deringhouse nodded.

'You've got to take your hat off to a man like that,' Rhodan said thoughtfully.

Deringhouse asked: 'What are your plans now, sir?'

Rhodan shrugged his shoulders and smiled. 'Nothing. They don't have a ship left with which to leave Venus. Maybe they'll manage to repair the transporter; then they won't have to walk. What do you think will become of them?'

'Do you believe that those men will be able to survive?' Deringhouse asked in doubt.

Rhodan nodded. 'Why not? One of them made it. How much easier it will be for them to do it to-gether!'

*

Shortly after they lifted off again, Rhodan instructed Tako Kakuta in the *Stardust* to perform his space leap.

A few days earlier – Terrestrial time – when Rhodan decided to spare the lives of Tomisenkov and his men, he had thereby automatically killed his other plan to rid Venus of the foreign intruders, thus demonstrating to the positronic brain that the threat had been eliminated and that it was safe to open the entrance.

Tako Kakuta, a Japanese like Son Okura and many other members of the Mutant Corps, was the only one among Rhodan's men who had the capacity of teleportation. Thanks to the development of his brain caused by mutation, it had the energy which enabled him to transport himself over distances up to 30,000 miles in a manner resembling the transition of a spaceship.

Therefore, Tako Kakuta was the only one who could succeed in penetrating the barrier with which the positronic brain had surrounded the Venus fortress to keep out all aliens.

Rhodan had considered this possibility before. Since it entailed a certain risk for the Japanese, he had preferred a different approach. Now he figured that survival of Tomisenkov's army was worth the risks involved for Kakuta and he did not hesitate to give the appropriate order to the Japanese who had already been prepared for his mission for some time.

The radius of the protective mantle around the fortress measured 300 miles. Even though he wore a transport suit, it would take quite a while till Kakuta could enter the proper fortifications.

*

Rhodan's men were on the verge of exhaustion after the strenuous days on the planet Wanderer followed by the uninterrupted action on Venus. This became evident in their almost childlike joy when the silhouette of the *Stardust* emerged over the horizon.

The transporters moved about 30 feet above the treetops of the jungle in their usual formation.

They had overcome all perils and the comfort of the giant vessel aroused pleasant expectations. A soft bed, a decent breakfast – none of those Arkonide rations – and most of all time to rest and play. These were good enough reasons to get excited.

Rhodan smiled and listened to the merry banter over the telecom.

Reginald Bell had made the arrangements for the return of the little expedition. They could see through their binoculars from 10 miles away that the huge door of the southern airlock was open.

Tako Kakuta had performed his space jump. He reported over the telecom, which was unaffected by the protective screen of the base, that he was on his way to the entrance of the fortress. Rhodan guessed that it would take at least another hour before Tako managed to obtain agreement from the positronic brain to lift the barrier.

*

'I've got it!' Capt. Liubol shouted enthusiastically.

He stared at the target screen of the neutron beamer and pulled the lever he assumed to be the trigger. At first nothing happened but in a few seconds the trees which showed on the screen burned to ashes.

Tomisenkov grunted happily. 'It was about time!' he said. 'Here they come!'

He looked at the observation screen which displayed the area northwest of the vehicle. The dark silhouette of the mighty sphere disturbed him and he could not suppress the thought that his plan was too reckless and that it was foolish to expose his men to such odds.

They had set the transporter into motion and attempted to find Rhodan's track. Instead of finding his track they had discovered the *Stardust*. They did not dare get close to the *Stardust* but they hoped to be able to intercept Rhodan and his group in the vicinity. Before they had depended only on their machineguns and mortars; but now – thanks to Capt. Liubol's constant experimentation – they had found out how to use the built-in weapons of the transporter.

This considerably increased their chance of success.

*

'Alarm!' the man at the micro-wave detector yelled.

But it was already too late.

The hull of the transporter began to crackle. Rhodan diagnosed the noise at once as a hit from a neutron beamer.

The craft and its occupants would have been lost, had it not been for Rhodan's unique capability to react within a fraction of a second to the most unexpected situations.

He jumped forward and grabbed the joystick over the shoulder of the pilot, who was scared stiff.

The transporter tilted and spun down the 30 feet into the foliage of the trees. Twigs and branches broke around it and when the vehicle came to rest it was buried 10 feet deep under the leaves and safely out of the sight of the aggressors.

The radiation monitor beeped continuously. The neutron-induced radioactivity exceeded the safe level.

Deringhouse reported in a monotone: 'Enemy sighted. Commence firing.'

Deringhouse's transporter let go with the impulse-beamer.

The first salvo would have made a lump of molten metal out of Tomisenkov's vehicle, had he not re-acted quick as a flash and pulled away after his bungled attempt to destroy the transporter leading the flight.

Deringhouse's shot caught Tomisenkov's machine in the tail. The rear end was the location of the gravity poles which were essential for the distribution of the neutral field. The transporter plopped down like a stone before Tomisenkov had a chance to make a maneuver to regain his balance.

There was a loud whoosh as the craft crashed through the foliage and Tomisenkov's head was thrown so hard against the instrument panel that he was instantly knocked out.

Meanwhile Rhodan had pushed the pilot out of his seat and taken over the controls. Through a gap in the leaves he saw the hostile vehicle plunge down, followed by another transporter.

'Deringhouse, is that you?'

'Yes, sir!' Deringhouse called. 'I won't let him get away!'

'Leave him alone!' Rhodan ordered sternly.

'But he's using our own weapons, sir!' Deringhouse protested.

'Never mind!'

Deringhouse came back and the transporters formed up again.

Rhodan gave a short report about the incident to the *Stardust* and added: 'Our vehicle and the occupants will have to be decontaminated. Have everything ready!'

Decontamination of radioactive bodies was a standard procedure on board the *Stardust*. As the refined product of an advanced technology, it was equipped for all such eventualities. The beeping of the radiation monitor ceased as soon as the transporter entered the decontamination shower.

*

Although he knew precisely how the positroni-computer would react to his unannounced entry into the fortress, Tako Kakuta, the Japanese teleporter, felt uneasy as he approached the control center of the mechanical brain through wide, brightly lit corridors inside the mountain.

He was under constant observation, there was no

doubt about it. There were plenty of cameras and microphones concealed in the walls.

When he had proceeded halfway into the mountain, the positronic brain had already detected his goal. The right wall of the corridor through which he walked opened up a few yards and from the opening emerged a group of robot guards who had watched over the security and maintenance of the fortress for thousands of years.

Tako offered no resistance. The robots led him away and took him through halls and in antigrav elevators deep down under the surface to a room which served as an investigation center. The cerebrotronic machine applied the most effective and safest method for its inquiry, namely hypnotic interrogation.

The inquiring machine could read Tako's mind like an open book and he had no control whatsoever over it. Tako gave the information that Perry Rhodan's last instructions should no longer be obeyed because they inflicted serious dangers to Rhodan himself.

The brain machine exercised its own judgment and acted accordingly.

It sent a message to the telecom receiver in the *Stardust* stating:

'THE DEFENSE SCREEN WILL BE OPENED FROM 173:00 O'CLOCK. ADMITTANCE DURING THIS INTERVAL.'

Rhodan was ready with his ship.

*

Capt. Liubol sat in the top of a giant tree to watch the *Stardust*. A second man sat close behind him to watch for flying reptiles and to protect Liubol from their attack while his eyes were trained on the battleship.

Gen. Tomisenkov – with a big lump and a smarting headache – kept asking impatiently from below what there was to see.

The fourth man of the team, an electronics technician, climbed all over the precariously balanced wreck in the branches and tried to determine whether it could be fixed up enough to do anything with it.

The *Stardust* presented a very imposing view; but when Liubol had waited half an hour and the gigantic sphere had not moved, he had the impression that he was wasting his time.

As a result of his examination the electronics technician had in the meantime come to some conclusions which drove Tomisenkov to despair.

The technician declared categorically that the essential parts of the transporter were damaged to such an extent that it would be impossible to put it back into operation without knowledge of the foreign technology.

'At least pull out the cannon Liubol fired before!' Tomisenkov growled.

'It's no use, sir,' the technician replied. 'All aggregates of the transporter and the weapons, too, drew their energy from a generator which sustained most of the damage.'

Tomisenkov did not want to believe him until the technician showed him the specific components in the vehicle and explained to him how they were damaged and how little anyone could know about the aliens' technology.

Only then did Tomisenkov realize that he had lost another round of the game – a round with extremely high stakes.

He understood now that he had to make peace on this world. Either they learned to cope with the environment on Venus or they wouldn't even live long enough for a rescue expedition to reach them.

'Liubol, come down!' Tomisenkov shouted. 'That vehicle,' he said with a disdainful gesture of his hand after he had assembled his men on the ground, 'is broken and out of commission. We'll have to work our way back to the camp on foot. It's going to be a tough march; but I've been able to do it alone, so the four of us should manage to get through. Liubol, take the compass and lead the way. The most important rules are: stick together and don't touch anything unless you have to. Let's go!'

At first they did not think it was too bad. The undergrowth was tangled and sometimes animals ran across their feet and made them feel queasy; but they moved along and made fairly good time.

Only when the sun began to set did they start to worry about the night which would last as long as five days on Earth: 120 hours in a dark jungle!

And the more they thought about it, the gloomier their future looked to them. They had no ships to leave this planet. They were condemned to spend the rest of their lives on Venus!

They did not talk for hours, lost in their melancholy thoughts.

But then two of the animals that resembled bears got wind of them. Liubol noticed them first and Tomiscnkov advised them how to deal with the beasts. Following his instructions they hid out in an ambush. When the animals, which were not too smart, stalked them and came close, they were killed with grenade rifles.

Then they marched on.

Before they reached their camp, they would have to fight many times. But their courage and a confident mood had returned; with it the burning pride to show the world that somebody had come who was mightier than the wilderness and its ponderous saurians, its huge reptiles and all its repulsive slimy worms.

Whatever they believed in, whatever the ideology they had learned, no matter with how much injustice they treated each other – they were human.

They were members of the proudest, most ambitious and daring race in the Galaxy.

And they would survive – not all of them, but enough so that the chain would never be broken.

*

The positronic brain processed the information from the curved segment of the Wanderer's orbit and predicted that the entire problem would be solved within the next two hours.

One more day and it would have been too late to ascertain the desired answer from the fragment.

For the first time Rhodan's face expressed his great relief. He called Col. Freyt in Galacto-City.

Freyt evidenced great relief when he learned that Rhodan and the *Stardust* would return to Earth in a few hours. 'You know, sir,' he confessed, 'more and more of our own people are failing to understand me. They ask me to take some action to contain the expansionist policies of the Eastern Bloc and I . . .'

Rhodan nodded. 'We'll take care of all that. Don't worry about it. Don't breathe a word to anybody about our arrival, right?'

Reginald Bell, who had listened in on the conversation, did not understand much of it. While the positronic brain was in the process of computing the Wanderer trajectory, Rhodan gave his explanation:

'When we left Earth, I did not know when we would return. I appointed Col. Freyt as my deputy;

but how well did I really know Freyt? How was I to know but what, with the tremendous power at his disposal, he wouldn't commit some foolish act at the first opportunity? I had to have absolute assurance. That's why Freyt was administered a hypno-block which forbade him to intervene in global politics. Moreover, a few mutants remained behind in Galacto-City who, in a sense, exercised thought control and made sure that he did not take any rash measures.

'As we can now see with hindsight, the idea of a hypno-block was based on a miscalculation on my part – or let's say, my opinion about the development of global politics was too optimistic. I considered the situation to be fairly stable. It didn't seem thinkable to me that anyone could still be interested or succeed in disrupting pan-terrestrial unity.' The Peacelord shrugged his shoulders. 'Otherwise Freyt would have received quite different instructions from me. As matters stand now, he is not permitted to do anything but repulse an attack on the Gobi base, should one be made. His hands have been tied in all other respects.'

'You mustn't reproach yourself.' Bell was sympathetic. 'Nobody could have foreseen that we'd be gone four and a half years.'

Rhodan shook his head. He was severe with himself, as usual. 'When you carry a responsibility as big as mine, Reg, you've got to consider all the contingencies all the time, no matter how unlikely they may seem.'

He elaborated on another case.

'We were up against the same problem with the fortress. I was too cautious; I didn't take into account that some people other than our own might land on Venus. The robot brain reacted as programmed: it did not interfere with *humans* – Tomisenkov and his men – and if we hadn't intervened in the nick of time, they probably would have occupied the base. It was only when Tomisenkov with his rockets started shooting at us that the robot brain registered 'unusual and alarming circumstances' and locked everybody out – including us.

'I've taken precautions to change this. In the future when there are ships with you or me and a few others select in them, we'll send a coded signal to the brain so that it will open its entrance in the most critical circumstances.'

'Thank you!' said Reg.

Perry was genuinely surprised. 'For what?'

'For the confidence.'

'Oh, you . . .' But Perry's reply was interrupted by a signal from the positronic brain. Its mechanical voice announced: 'RESULT AVAILABLE IN 50 MINUTES.'

Bell got up. 'What are we going to do now?'

Rhodan's face suddenly became very serious, very determined. 'I think we've shown patience long enough,' he said with quiet resolve. 'If the people of Earth haven't the sense, the will, the ability – if they don't *want* to be united – they'll have to be for their own good. We can't afford to move out into the universe with the threat of disunity at our back. We must make a clean sweep and we'll start with the troublemakers.'

As he spoke his last words, a volcano in the west began to give signs of imminent eruption. 'An omen!' said Rhodan.

Propelled by tremendous internal pressure, from inside Venus a gigantic molten column of glowing yellow magma was ejected into the atmosphere. Hundreds of yards it rose, a brimstone barrage of extra-terrestrial pyrotechnics that illuminated the twilit land with an eerie phosphorescent light.

'A beacon in the night,' Bell murmured.